Sonoran
Sweetheart

*Also by Nancy J. Farrier
in Large Print:*

Tucson: Sonoran Sunrise
Tucson: Sonoran Star

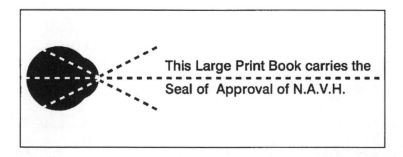

Sonoran Sweetheart

Nancy J. Farrier

Thorndike Press • Waterville, Maine

Published in 2006 by arrangement with
Barbour Publishing, Inc.

Thorndike Press® Large Print Candlelight.

The tree indicium is a trademark of Thorndike Press.

The text of this Large Print edition is unabridged.
Other aspects of the book may vary from the original edition.

Set in 16 pt. Plantin by Elena Picard.

Printed in the United States on permanent paper.

Library of Congress Cataloging-in-Publication Data

Farrier, Nancy J.
    [Sonoran sweetheart]
    Tucson. Sonoran sweetheart : a romance in the Old
Southwest / by Nancy J. Farrier.
        p. cm. — (Tucson ; #3) (Thorndike Press large print
Candlelight)
    Originally published: Sonoran sweetheart. Uhrichsville,
Ohio : Heartsong Presents, 2002.
    ISBN 0-7862-8419-6 (lg. print : hc : alk. paper)
    1. Religious fiction. I. Title. II. Thorndike Press large
print Candlelight series.
PS3556.A77276S67 2006
  813'.6—dc22   2005036798

Sonoran Sweetheart

National Association for Visually Handicapped
serving the partially seeing

As the Founder/CEO of NAVH, the only national health agency solely devoted to those who, although not totally blind, have an eye disease which could lead to serious visual impairment, I am pleased to recognize Thorndike Press* as one of the leading publishers in the large print field.

Founded in 1954 in San Francisco to prepare large print textbooks for partially seeing children, NAVH became the pioneer and standard setting agency in the preparation of large type.

Today, those publishers who meet our standards carry the prestigious "Seal of Approval" indicating high quality large print. We are delighted that Thorndike Press is one of the publishers whose titles meet these standards. We are also pleased to recognize the significant contribution Thorndike Press is making in this important and growing field.

Lorraine H. Marchi, L.H.D.
Founder/CEO
NAVH

* Thorndike Press encompasses the following imprints: Thorndike, Wheeler, Walker and Large Print Press.

Chapter 1

Arizona Territory, 1870s

The ring of the blacksmith's hammer striking against hot metal reverberated through the air, making Lavette Johnson's heart pound in time to the beat. Like primitive, rhythmic music, the sound drew her, intoxicating and unavoidable. She moved to the doorway of the shop, past horses waiting at the hitching post, neat piles of tools, and various utensils waiting for repair. Extra aprons for protection against heat and sparks hung on hooks by the door. A workbench with a variety of hammers and tools laid in orderly rows stood along one side of the three-sided room.

Stepping out of the bright sunlight, Lavette squinted against the dimness of the forge. She blinked, then stared at the giant of a man who swung the huge hammer as if it were a child's toy. His shirt, the sleeves torn and frayed at the shoulders, clung like a second skin to his bulging muscles. The blacksmith switched the hammer into his other hand and didn't lose a beat. His ebony skin glistened, the glow of the fire in the forge making tiny light particles dance across his arms.

Lavette sucked in a breath, pulling hard to get more air. Black dots danced across her vision. In a recess of her mind, she wondered if this was the way Miss Susannah felt before she swooned in order to get some handsome boy's attention. Lavette shoved the thought away. She didn't like to remember the years she'd spent as a slave to Miss Susannah's family before her people were liberated at the end of the war. Free! She scoffed at the word. She would never be free. She wasn't then, and she wasn't now. Lavette refused to listen to people talk about emancipation. She'd resigned herself to a life of servitude in one form or another. She didn't understand why she had to be in bondage, but she knew her place.

She also knew she had no room in her life for a husband or children. She'd seen what happened to her papa and mama when their older sons and daughters were sold off one by one, many of them leaving while they were still too young to be separated from their parents.

"We need to do this while they're young enough to train right," Miss Susannah's papa said. Lavette didn't believe a word of it. He was cruel and greedy, only looking at the money he would make from the sale. He always seemed to delight in the weeping and moaning of the parting relatives.

Unable to take her eyes off the man working at the forge, Lavette knew she had to leave. This blacksmith had been recommended as the best, but Lavette knew better now. He was a dangerous man. Oh, he probably was the best in Tucson, but her heart could tell he was a threat to her. The sight of him heightened her senses. She used to dream about the kind of man she would marry. Of course, that was before she knew she would never be a wife. This man with his great height, treelike arms, and good reputation fulfilled all her girlish dreams. She always imagined a big, strong husband who could shelter her from all the pain of life. Part of her longed to race forward in excited anticipation, the other part desired to race away in absolute terror.

Terror won. Lavette stepped back to

make an exit. Her movement must have caught the blacksmith's eye, for he looked up. Like a rabbit caught in a snare, she froze. Intelligence shone from his black eyes along with something else she couldn't quite name. He stared, his hammer poised for a blow that never fell. Now that he faced her, she could see he was as handsome as she'd dreamed he would be, with rounded cheeks and a slightly flattened nose. His face split in a wide grin. Lavette couldn't breathe. Oh, she was right. This was a dangerous man.

Josiah Washington usually lost himself in the rhythm of his work. Once, he'd loved the solitude and the pounding beat of the hammer falling on the metal. During these times he felt closest to Jesus. Lately, he'd needed that closeness. Although he had friends in Tucson, an ache of loneliness had begun to needle at him. He watched his friends Lieutenant Conlon Sullivan and his wife Glorianna, and now Deputy Quinn Kirby had married Kathleen O'Connor. They were so happy. They shared something special between them. Every time he saw them together, Josiah couldn't stop the heart-wrenching anguish that filled him.

Shame filled him. He should be thankful to God for the friends he had. Before he'd led Conlon to the Lord, he'd had no friends as such. Since then, he'd become close with the Sullivans, the Kirbys, and friendly with the other Christians who worshipped with them. These believers agreed with I Samuel 16:7. Instead of looking at his skin color, they looked at his heart. He should be content with that.

Jesus, I don't mean to complain, but I'm tired of being alone. If this is Your will that I remain single all my life, then please remove the desire I have for a wife. But, Lord, if You have someone in mind, let me know clearly when I see her. Thank You, Jesus.

With a lithe movement, Josiah slipped the hammer from his right hand to his left. He hated the thought of ending up with one arm bigger than the other like some blacksmiths did. When his father taught him to shoe horses, he also showed him the trick of working the metal with either hand. Josiah made sure to keep in constant practice.

Something moved at the front of the shop. Josiah looked up, expecting to see one of his regular customers bringing him a new job. He'd never lacked for work since leaving the cavalry and coming to Tucson. Some of the other blacksmiths complained because their steady customers preferred Josiah's work to theirs. He didn't intend to take away their clients, but he wouldn't compromise his work ethics, either.

The heat from the hot metal he was working rose in undulating waves in front of him. A mirage. That's what he was seeing. She certainly wasn't one of his regulars. Delicate bone structure gave her heart-shaped face an ethereal look. Her flawless complexion, dark coffee with a touch of milk, made his fingers twitch with a longing to touch. Josiah's chest began to ache. He realized he'd been holding his breath. He exhaled and drew in a deep, ragged breath. This was the woman of his dreams, the woman God made to be a helpmeet for him. Oh, that she could be real and not a vision.

She moved. Josiah caught his breath. She took another small step backwards. Suddenly he knew she wasn't a mirage, vision, or dream. She was real — a living, breathing person. *God, is this Your answer? Is she the one?*

Josiah's hammer clattered to the floor. They both jumped. He hadn't even realized he was losing his grip on the heavy tool. He glanced down at the iron scraps the hammer had fallen on, feeling stupid as he tried to pull his thoughts together. When he looked back at the door, she had stepped close enough to it to be framed by the bright sun. Wisps of curly black fizzed out from the rest of her hair, which was pulled back into a neat bun at the base of her neck. A look of uncertainty or fear widened her already large eyes. A burst of compassion such as Josiah had never known raced through him. He wanted nothing more than to care for this woman and to protect her from whatever she feared.

She turned to leave.

"Wait." Josiah stretched out his hand, wishing he could reach across and stop her. Panic rose up at the thought that she might go, and he would never have the chance to find out her name.

She hesitated, her face still turned away.

Stepping around the bench, Josiah closed the distance between them in two quick strides. In slow motion, she twisted back around to face him. The scents of cinnamon, fresh bread, and wood smoke wafted up from her.

"Cinnamon."

"What?" The vision's melodic voice matched the rest of her.

Horrified, Josiah realized he'd spoken his thoughts aloud. "I, uh." He glanced around, hoping to come up with something that would sound plausible. He didn't. Josiah shrugged. The truth was always best anyway. "You smell like cinnamon."

She looked down, her impossibly long eyelashes brushing like delicate butterflies against her cheeks. Josiah was in the act of lifting his hand to touch her face when he caught himself. What was he doing? He didn't even know her name. For some reason, he couldn't think clearly. Frantic that she would disappear, he struggled to think of something to say. Why was she here?

"Oh." Josiah's gasp of the word caused the angel to look up. "Is there something I could help you with, Miss?"

"Johnson." A small smile flitted across her lips.

Josiah stared at her. He couldn't figure out what she was saying. He couldn't remember what he'd asked.

"Lavette Johnson. My name is Lavette Johnson." She tilted her head back and managed to look at him. Even her eyes reminded him of spices. The rich brown depths glowed with intelligence and humor.

"Josiah. Washington." Josiah knew she must think him a complete dolt. He couldn't drag his gaze from the multitude of wiry strands of hair framing her face like a troop of fairies dancing in pure joy at her beauty. He could feel from the stretching of his cheeks that he must be grinning at her, but he couldn't seem to quit.

Lavette took a step away, then held out her hand. "It's a pleasure to meet ya, Mr. Washington."

For the first time, he noticed her pronounced Southern accent. He thought he could listen to her talk all day, even if she never said anything even halfway important.

"We don't stand on much formality out here." Josiah did his best to scale down the overpowering grin to a smile. "You can call me Josiah."

Once more, her eyelashes rested on the gentle slope of her cheek. "I don't believe I know you well enough for that, Mr. Washington. Perhaps if we become friends, I will consider using your given name."

Friends? Had she said they might become friends? Josiah wanted to do cartwheels like that young fellow who worked at that sideshow had done.

"Hey, Smithy."

Josiah tensed. Even the smile left his face. He straightened and turned toward the opening of his shop. Bertrand Mead. He'd know that voice anywhere. One of the drawbacks of being in business was the necessity of serving the public, no matter how difficult they were. Bertrand Mead was worse than difficult. Mead owned a hostelry and saloon. To all intents and purposes, he gave the appearance of being a well-to-do businessman. Josiah knew differently. He knew about the secret houses Mead was suspected of running. There was even talk about him bringing in young girls from back East to work there — girls too young to work anywhere except doing chores for their mama or papa. The thought of such an immoral action made Josiah's blood boil.

Stepping around Miss Johnson, Josiah nodded at the fancy-dressed man seated in a small buggy. "What can I do for you, Mr. Mead?" Josiah's voice must have held a warning, for Lavette moved a step closer, like she was trying to hide behind him.

"I want you to take a look at my team." Mead gestured at the matched bays hitched to his buggy. "They haven't been shod in awhile. I think the mare is getting ready to throw a shoe."

Standing several feet away from the horses, Josiah could still hear the faint click of a loose shoe as the mare fidgeted. "Would you like me to stop by and get the horses, or do you want to leave them now? I can take care of them as soon as I finish the job I'm working on, if you like." Although he didn't care about pleasing this customer, Josiah did his best to keep contact with Mead to a minimum. The faster he finished the man's horses, the sooner he could be out of his oily presence.

"I have a little business down the street, so I'll leave them now." Mead stepped down, landing gingerly in the dust, careful of his polished shoes. He brushed imaginary dirt from his pant leg, then tossed the lead rope toward Josiah. The mare jerked her head away, white showing around her eyes. In one swift move, Josiah swept up the rope. He stepped closer and began to soothe the startled horse, wondering if Mead abused the animal to have her react like that.

"Well, well, what have we here?"

Josiah whirled around at Mead's question. He'd forgotten that stepping toward

17

the mare would expose Miss Johnson. When he moved, she was no longer concealed from Mead's sight.

Lavette stared at the ground in front of her. Her hands clenched the folds of her skirt. Small white teeth caught at her bottom lip to keep it from quivering. She looked terrified. Josiah understood. The Southern accent. The hesitance at meeting his eyes. She'd once been a slave. She knew the power a white man had over a black girl. No wonder she was so scared.

Wrapping the lead rein around the hitching post, Josiah let his long stride carry him between Mead and Miss Johnson. "I'll have those horses ready for you in an hour, Mr. Mead. You can go ahead and take care of your business."

Mead moved to the side of Josiah. His shifty gaze traveled over Miss Johnson in a way that made Josiah want to wipe Mead's face in the dirt. *Vengeance is mine, saith the Lord.* Josiah wanted to groan as the verse popped into his head. Most of the time he found it easy to allow the Lord to work. Right now, he wanted to take over and do things his way rather than wait for God to handle matters.

"I don't believe I've met this young lady." Bertrand looked at Josiah. His ice blue eyes glinted with an evil look. "Perhaps you could introduce us."

Clenching his teeth, Josiah stepped to Lavette's side. "Miss Johnson, this is Bertrand Mead. Mead, Miss Johnson."

Mead bowed low, sweeping the hat from his head. "This is truly a pleasure, Miss Johnson. I'm sure I can't wait to get to know you better." He lifted her hand to his lips.

With a small cry, Lavette yanked her hand back. Lifting her skirts, she raced away down the street.

Chapter 2

Closing the kitchen door behind her, Lavette leaned back against the wood, her legs trembling so hard, she wondered how she managed to make her way home. She'd gone from total elation to complete terror so fast, her mind was still catching up to her body. When Bertrand Mead had touched her, all she could feel were the times Miss Susannah's father would catch her alone and put his slimy hands on her. She shuddered. Bile rose in her throat. What was she to do? Would Mr. Mead find out where she lived?

Her breathing slowed, and Lavette made her way to the bucket of water by the stove. Wetting her face, she thought how nice it would be to wash away her troubles as well. She hadn't been around Master Brennan, Susannah's father, in nine years, yet she could still see and feel him as if he were here in this room. Growing up, she'd lived in terror of the man. Even when she was a young girl, Mr. Brennan would look at her in a way that made her uncomfortable. As she grew older, she learned to never be near him without Miss Susannah close by.

"Lavette? Are you here?" A thin, quavery voice came through the doorway, followed by deep, hacking coughs. A bell tinkled.

Lavette dried her face and hurried to the front bedroom where Mrs. Sawyer rested. The elderly woman lay on her side, her translucent skin taking on a slightly bluish cast. She held a handkerchief to her mouth as the coughs racked her frail body. Her gray-white hair, flattened on one side, curled around her face.

Moving to the basin of water on the night table, Lavette wet a clean rag to wipe the perspiration from Mrs. Sawyer's brow. The features on the left side of Mrs. Sawyer's face still sagged a little, refusing to work properly just as her left arm and leg gave her problems. Eight months ago Lavette had come home from shopping to find Mrs. Sawyer lying on the floor, pale as death. The doctor diagnosed the problem as apoplexy. He assured Lavette that her mistress might improve, but the improvements would be slow and would take a lot of work. Then he showed Lavette how to help Mrs. Sawyer exercise her limbs and suggested she encourage her to talk, even though the sounds were garbled.

For the first few weeks, Lavette felt nothing but despair as she tried to help the kind lady. The muscles refused to respond. Mrs. Sawyer couldn't seem to say the simplest words that once flowed with ease. As the day wore on and she tired, the responses were smaller. By evening, Mrs. Sawyer would be in tears, and Lavette often felt like joining her.

Lavette refused to give up on the exercises and made Mrs. Sawyer repeat certain words every day. Bit by bit, she began to improve. Now, after eight long months, her speech faltered only a little, and she walked a short distance with Lavette's assistance. Her movements were still very slow, but even the doctor praised them both for the progress they'd made. It hadn't been easy coming out here. They'd taken the trip in short distances, and each day had taken its toll. Still, they'd made it. Now, although she had a nasty cold, Mrs. Sawyer seemed to be gaining strength.

"Is Gretta coming by today?" Mrs. Sawyer's gaze sought Lavette's.

"She'll be here in time for the evening meal." Lavette forced a smile and a light tone, not wanting Mrs. Sawyer to know the horror she'd faced this morning. After all, this woman wouldn't understand the terror and the power white men had over her.

"I need to get up and dressed." Mrs. Sawyer's voice was hoarse from all the coughing. Sweat popped out on her brow as she tried to sit up unassisted.

"Not yet." Lavette put her arm behind Mrs. Sawyer for support as she plumped the pillows and piled them behind her. Then she eased the older lady back until she rested against the cushioning. "Dinner is a long way off. You need to rest so you'll be ready for those rambunctious grandsons of yours."

Mrs. Sawyer's pale blue eyes lit with some of their old sparkle. "They are quite a rowdy trio. I wish I felt good enough to get up and run with them. Why are they coming so late?"

"Your son-in-law will be able to join you for tonight's meal. Your daughter will be here in the afternoon with the children, then he will join you at dinnertime."

Mrs. Sawyer gave Lavette a smile that shone with sincerity. "He's such a wonderful young man and so good to Gretta and the children."

"I'm sure he's as wonderful as you say."

Lavette finished straightening the covers.

"I'll bring you some breakfast, then you can rest for awhile." Lavette hurried to the kitchen, having noted the tired circles beneath her mistress's eyes. She wouldn't be awake for long and needed some nourishing food to continue gaining strength.

The familiarity of the routine gave Lavette time to think as she worked. Her thoughts strayed back to this morning, to the time before that repulsive Mead had accosted her. Instead, she could clearly recall the blacksmith's warm smile and dark eyes. Had his eyes shone with interest in her? Her pulse quickened, and for a moment, she allowed the childhood dream of husband and family to wash over her. She imagined the patter of bare feet racing across the floor and the eager smiles on the small faces. Those smiles all resembled the friendly grin of a certain blacksmith.

With a final tap, Josiah finished the last shoe on Bertrand Mead's mare. He patted her, rubbing down her neck and scratching her ears. She sure was a sweet horse. If he ever found out Mead was mistreating her, he'd take her away from the man. No one should be allowed to own animals if he abused them.

"Have you finished?"

Josiah turned around at the sound of Bertrand Mead's voice. The bay pressed close against Josiah's side.

"Yes, Sir." Josiah patted the mare's neck, hoping to reassure her. She tried to dance away as Mead stepped closer.

Mead raised the short buggy whip, his eyes flashing with anger. "Stupid horse. I should sell her and get a decent one."

"Would you like me to hitch her to the buggy?" Josiah stepped in front of the mare, hoping to keep Mead from hitting her.

"Fine. See to it." Mead crossed to stand in the shade near his buggy, the whip flicking against his leg in a steady rhythm.

Doing his best to soothe the skittish mare, Josiah urged her back into the traces next to the other bay. Her eyes rolled as she tilted her head to keep an eye on her owner. Nostrils wide, she snorted and stamped, the opposite of the sweet, contented horse he'd finished shoeing.

"There you go, Sir." Josiah strode to her head to give her a final pat as Mead climbed into the buggy. "She's a fine animal. They make a smart-looking team."

"Of course they do." Mead's icy gaze chilled Josiah. "I wouldn't have anything less." He leaned forward, his gaze riveting. "Speaking of smart looking, who was the young lady with you earlier?"

"I introduced you to her." Josiah wanted to walk away and ignore the question. He could picture slime dripping from this man.

"Yes, I remember her name." Mead slapped the whip against the side of the conveyance, causing both horses to jump. Mead jerked the reins. "I want to know who she is, where she lives."

Josiah breathed a silent sigh of relief. At least he could answer honestly. "I only met her this morning. I don't know where she stays."

Mead's pale eyes fastened on Josiah's with a gaze that would have intimidated many men. A slow, feral smile tilted his lips but didn't reach his eyes. "I have plans for that girl. You don't often find beauty like hers." His eyes took on a thoughtful gaze. "I wonder if she can sing as pretty as she looks. Imagine what she would do for my business. Of course, there are other ways a beautiful girl can be useful."

Anger swept through Josiah. He clenched his fists tightly against his legs. Every part of him wanted to drag this man from the buggy and wipe that insolent look from his face. *Vengeance is mine.* The voice of the Holy Spirit seemed to whisper in his mind. The anger drained away, and Josiah stepped back to watch Mead drive off, whipping his horses to a quick trot.

Stalking back into the shop, Josiah stoked the fire, then picked up his hammer. The heavy instrument felt good as his fist tightened around the handle. He couldn't wait for the ore to get pliable in the heat. Was this why the Lord made him a blacksmith — so he could take out his anger and frustrations on metal instead of pounding men like Mead?

Stirring the coals, Josiah shoved a piece of iron in to heat up. Impatience tore at him, making him want to pull the rod from the fire long before it would be ready. At last, he plucked the bar out, shaking the remnants of red-hot coals from the shaft. After swinging over to the anvil, Josiah hefted the hammer in his hand and began to pound with a vengeance that sent sparks flying.

Jesus, help me. You know I want to think about this being Mead instead of a piece of iron. Help me to forgive, to find something about the man that is lovable in Your eyes. I surely can't see anything from my point of view.

The redness faded as the bar cooled, and Josiah turned to thrust it back into the coals for a second heating. He did feel better. Praying and working always helped. Blacksmithing was a noisy occupation and gave him plenty of time for prayer and thinking.

When he finished talking with God, his mind strayed from Bertrand Mead to Lavette Johnson. Never had he seen such a beautiful woman. He could picture Adam's reaction to Eve in the garden when Adam said, "This is now bone of my bones, flesh of my flesh." Adam must have been as bowled over by Eve as Josiah was with Lavette. She had to be the one for him. He could still remember the prayer, then looking up and seeing her.

"I don't think I've ever seen anyone so excited over his work before. Have you, Quinn?" Conlon Sullivan stood in the door of the shop next to Deputy Quinn Kirby. Both of them had thoughtful expressions on their faces.

"Nope. I don't believe I have." Quinn frowned and shook his head. "I love my job, and I know you love yours, but we don't go around wearing a grin that stretches our cheeks out of shape while we're doing our work."

Heat other than from the forge warmed Josiah's face. He put the metal bar back by the coals, trying to give himself some time to get over the embarrassment of being caught thinking of Lavette. At least with his dark skin, his cheeks wouldn't show red like Quinn's usually did. He wiped his hands on a rag.

"Afternoon, Conlon, Quinn. What brings you over this way? Got time to sit a spell?" Gesturing at a bench outside in the shade, Josiah waited for the pair to lead the way, then followed.

Conlon slumped down and tilted his hat forward to lessen the sun's brightness. "We may not have come for anything in particular. That bright light drew us."

"That's right." Quinn pretended to rub his eyes. "The glow from your smithy made the sun look dim for awhile. We didn't realize you could make a place shine like that."

"If Glorianna and I ever run out of lamp oil, we'll have you come over and light up the house."

"All right." Josiah thought about tipping the bench over and sending his joking friends into the dust. "If you don't want me to dunk you in the horse trough, lay off."

"Did you hear that, Deputy? I believe this man is threatening us."

Quinn frowned. "I may have to consult the judge on this one. I'm not sure of the penalty here."

Josiah laughed. He couldn't help it. These two were his friends, and they wouldn't quit until they wormed every bit of information from him they could. "Aw, what do you guys really want? A tool repaired? Horses shod?"

Blue eyes twinkled as Conlon chuckled. "I did have some business, but now we want to know the reason for that idiotic grin. A smile that dazzling doesn't come along every day."

With a groan, Josiah shook his head. Conlon wouldn't give up until he told him. They'd been friends for too long. He couldn't hide anything anymore.

"A girl came by the shop this morning." Warmth flowed through Josiah at the thought of Lavette.

"A girl?" Conlon raised an eyebrow. "Just any girl? Is this someone we know?"

"Naw. She's new in town. I don't even know where I can find her. She ran off before I could find out where she's living."

"If she's that afraid of you, maybe you should give up before you start." Conlon's remark started Quinn chuckling.

"She wasn't afraid of me. Bertrand Mead showed up."

Quinn and Conlon sobered. Quinn frowned. "He's enough to make anyone run away. I wish I could find something to pin on him, but that fella is slipperier than a wet snake."

Clapping Josiah on the back, Conlon nodded. "So tell us what you know about this girl."

"Her name is Lavette Johnson. She's the most beautiful woman God ever made." Josiah gave a sheepish grin. "I'm not saying Glorianna and Kathleen aren't beautiful, but Lavette is special. From her Southern accent and the way she acted around Mead, I'd say she grew up on a plantation as a slave."

"Did Mead do something wrong?" Quinn asked.

"Everything Mead does is wrong." Josiah groaned. "Sorry. I have a hard time finding something likable about that fella. Anyway, he was cocky and tried to touch her. She ran away."

"Did he go after her?" Quinn had a mean look in his eye.

"No, he let her go, but he knows her name, and he wants to find her. Who knows what he'll do if he does?"

"Well, I guess you'll have to find Miss Johnson before Mead does." Conlon stood and stretched. "If I wasn't needing to get business over with, I'd take the time to tell you all about the man in my regiment whose mother-in-law came to town with a servant who used to be a slave."

Chapter 3

Surging to his feet, Josiah didn't know whether to grab Conlon and hug him or shake him. "You know where she lives?"

"How many head of horses did you need shod, Conlon?" Quinn pulled out his knife and began to clean his fingernails.

"That's right." Conlon snapped his fingers. "Josiah, I wanted to see how soon you can come to Fort Lowell and check the horses. Several of them need new shoes before we go out on maneuvers again." Conlon studied the cloudless blue sky.

Josiah knew they were funning with him, so he bit back a groan. "I have to know where she lives. Tell me the man's name." Josiah wanted to get down on his knees and beg Conlon at the same time his stomach clenched in anticipation.

"Now, Josiah, you know I'm not a gossiping man. I'll have to go back and check with the gentleman involved and see if I can give out that information."

"Conlon, I will never shoe your horse again if you don't stop this."

"Josiah's a mite touchy, wouldn't you say, Quinn?"

"I will tell Glorianna, and you won't have a hot meal or a moment of peace for weeks." Josiah leaned forward, his fists on his hips.

Conlon winced. "Aw, you're getting downright mean." He sighed. "All right. I wouldn't want you bothering Glory about this, and I can see you're determined. Paul Ashton's mother-in-law arrived two weeks ago. She's had an attack of apoplexy, and his wife wanted her to come here to visit since they couldn't go back East. I think she's hoping her mother will decide to stay."

"So where are they living?" Josiah once again resisted the urge to shake the information out of Conlon.

"I don't know that." Conlon lifted his hat, ran his hand through his thick black hair, and settled his cap back on his head.

"What do you mean, you don't know?"

"Paul told us about them coming, but they aren't staying at the same house because Paul has three very rambunctious boys. They thought his mother-in-law

34

would be able to rest easier in a separate house."

Josiah groaned. "Where can I find this Paul Ashton so I can ask where they're living?"

"He'll be out at the fort all day. Then I believe he said something about coming to town for supper tonight." Conlon grinned and clapped Josiah on the back. "I'll ask him tomorrow, so when you come to shoe the horses, I can tell you where to find your lady."

"That might be too late." Josiah rubbed a drip of sweat from his temple.

"Why are you so certain you need to find her right away?" Quinn snapped his knife shut and slipped it back into his pocket.

"You didn't see the way Mead looked at her or hear the comments he made about her. That man has something in mind, and I don't think it's anything good."

Sauntering after Conlon, Quinn swung up onto his horse. He grinned at Conlon and gave him a wink. "You know that little adobe house about a block from Mrs. Monroy's boardinghouse?" Josiah felt a surge of hope as Quinn continued. "It's the house that sits back a ways from the road and has been deserted for several months."

Frowning, Conlon gave a quick nod.

"Yeah, I remember the place."

"I heard the other day that someone moved in there. Some lady from back East who's convalescing. I believe she has someone there helping her out."

Josiah let out a whoop. "I could drag you off that horse and hug you, Quinn Kirby. Of course, that's right after I yell at the two of you for tormenting me like this."

"I think that means we should leave." Quinn laughed and urged his horse after Conlon's.

"I'll be out to the fort on Thursday, Conlon," Josiah called after the two riders, the grin once more splitting his face. This afternoon, when he'd finished his work, he'd clean up, mosey over to that house, and welcome those newcomers. He'd show them the people of Tucson were mighty hospitable. He chuckled to himself. At least he wanted to show one of them how friendly he could be.

Straightening from putting away the last of the dishes, Lavette put her hands on her hips and rotated her shoulders to ease the ache. Moving Mrs. Sawyer around in the bed got harder every day. The older woman was gaining strength and weight. At times like tonight when Lavette's back felt like she'd been kicked by a whole herd of mules, she had to wonder if Mrs. Sawyer's continued recovery wasn't a mixed blessing. Shaking her head, she sighed as she wiped a few errant crumbs from the table. She'd come to care for Amelia Sawyer too much to want her to stay sickly. For years, she'd wanted to hate the woman but couldn't because Mrs. Sawyer had to be one of the most caring people she'd ever been around. Once Mrs. Sawyer believed a person worthwhile, she was very loyal to them.

Glancing out the window, Lavette could see the sun sinking lower in the sky, but still giving plenty of light. What would have been fall days back home proved to still carry summer warmth here in Tucson. A gentle breeze blew outside, and she relished the idea of sitting on the porch with the mending she intended to do this evening. That breeze would feel good, and she knew the house sat far enough from the street that most people wouldn't notice her. She had no desire to have anyone stop by for a conversation with her. She preferred the peace and quiet of her own thoughts after a day such as this one. Fixing supper and helping with Gretta's children while the adults ate always wore her out. Those boys were terrors, although adorable ones.

Settling into the chair at the end of the porch nearest the parlor, Lavette tipped her head back, allowing the soothing wind to cool her face. From here, she could hear her employer if she needed anything; yet with the trellis and vines coming down over the porch, she wouldn't be easily visible to those passing by. This position was almost as good as the weeping willow she used to sit under as a child, trying to hide from the ugliness of slavery.

Her thoughts turned to her family so far away. She hadn't seen them in years. By now her brother Toby would be eighteen. Was he married? Did he still work with her father, or had he moved out on his own? Lila and Nellie, her sisters, would be fourteen and eleven now. Lila would be starting to attract the attention of some of the young men in the area. Before long, they would be all grown up, and Lavette would have missed watching it happen. She blinked back tears, knowing they did no good and hating the weakness of them.

Placing her mending in her lap, Lavette watched the street. This small cottage sat back from the road, the view partially blocked by the large house in front of and to the side of this one. Although only a small portion of the roadway was visible, Lavette could see a few people strolling past. Evenings here seemed to be a time of getting out and visiting with neighbors. She was thankful her distance from the street gave her privacy.

A low moan came from inside the house. Lavette jumped up and set the skirt she was working on in the vacated chair. Walking quietly, she moved into the house and peeked into Mrs. Sawyer's room. The elderly woman had thrown off her covers, drawing her knees up to fight a chill. After tucking the blankets back around the woman, Lavette smoothed Mrs. Sawyer's hair and waited until her breathing evened. She tiptoed from the room. Quite often since they'd traveled west, Mrs. Sawyer woke from dreams that made her restless. Lavette hoped this wouldn't be one of those nights, or she wouldn't get much sleep, either.

The shadows were growing when Lavette stepped back out onto the porch. Her slippers whispered soft against the boards as she headed for her chair. When she bent to pick up her sewing, a shadow at the edge of the porch moved. Lavette clapped her hand across her mouth to avoid a shriek that would surely wake Mrs. Sawyer. Her heart pounded.

"Sorry to startle you, Miss Johnson. I saw you go inside. You left your mending on the chair, so I figured you'd be back out. I hope you don't mind that I waited." The huge blacksmith's grin banished the shadows.

Forcing herself to take a few deep breaths, Lavette waited a moment for her heart rate to slow. "You scared the insides out of me."

He twisted the hat in his hands until she wondered if the thing would survive the torture. "You rushed off so fast this morning, I didn't find out what you needed." Josiah looked chagrined, as if he knew the story sounded contrived. "Is there something I can do for you?"

Clasping her hands together, Lavette hoped Josiah wouldn't notice her trembling. For some strange reason, she couldn't control her emotions around this man. She couldn't even seem to concentrate on what he asked.

"Excuse me?" She felt stupid, staring at his wonderful smile and missing what he'd said.

"I wondered if there were some business I could help you with."

"I — uh, no I don't believe so."

He frowned, the fading of his smile allowing the shadows to close in. He arched one eyebrow. "Are you sure? You must have come by my shop for some reason. Do you have a horse that needs to be shod?"

A horse? His shop? Her brain tried to grasp his question. Remembrance flooded over her. "Oh, this morning." Heat suffused her cheeks. "I wanted to ask about a few things. They weren't important."

"Please sit down." He gestured at her still-vacant chair. Picking up her mending, she slid into the chair. His smile returned. Her heart sped up.

"If those things you wanted to ask about were important this morning, then they're still important now. Why don't you tell me what you need, and I'll see if I can help?"

"I — we arrived in Tucson a couple of weeks ago. Mrs. Sawyer plans to stay another six weeks. I wanted to inquire about getting a knife repaired and possibly getting another one to use while we're here. I thought perhaps you made tools as well as shoeing horses." She twisted the torn skirt in her hands until the prick of the needle stuck in the cloth startled her.

"I have several knives and other utensils

41

at my shop. I'll see that you get what you need." Josiah settled his large frame back against the rail, which creaked under the pressure.

"We'll only be here a short time before heading back East." Lavette couldn't meet his eyes. Maybe his interest would be discouraged if he thought she would be leaving soon.

"There's no reason your stay can't be as comfortable as possible." Josiah's voice was a deep rumble that calmed her. No wonder the man was so good with horses. She thought she could sit and listen to him talk all night. He spoke in such a slow, easy manner.

"I've heard you're here to visit Paul Ashton and his family. Where do you come from?" Josiah's eyes gleamed like obsidian in the shadows.

"We came here from Virginia." Lavette lowered her gaze from his, unable to meet his intense study for long.

"Have you always lived there?" Josiah crossed his arms over his massive chest. He acted like he planned to stay for a long time. Lavette couldn't think of a way to get rid of him fast without being offensive, and she didn't want to insult this gentle giant.

"I lived in Alabama before moving north

with Mrs. Sawyer because of her health." Smoothing the skirt she was mending, Lavette couldn't seem to quit talking so he would leave. "Mrs. Sawyer had to leave the South because of the damp in the air. The doctor said the moist night air was bad for her lungs, and the only hope for her to improve was to get her up north in the cooler, dryer climates. He wanted her to go to New York, but she insisted she didn't know anyone there. Her brother lived in Virginia, so we moved in with him."

"So when Mrs. Sawyer leaves, she'll return to her brother's house?"

Lavette's gaze jerked up to meet those twinkling eyes and that wide grin that affected her. She looked back down at her sewing. Had he meant to suggest she might not be returning with Mrs. Sawyer? If so, he didn't understand her position here. She had no choice about what she would do.

"Mrs. Sawyer's brother passed on last year. He never married. His solicitor has instructions to see that she is well cared for as long as she chooses to reside there. We'll be going back to Virginia as soon as this visit is over." Lavette wanted to ask Josiah to tell her about his background, if for no other reason than to hear his voice, but she didn't want him to think her interested. She wanted to discourage him, not encourage him.

"Tucson is a lot different than the cities in Virginia." Josiah shifted, uncrossing his arms and resting more on the porch rail. "Do you prefer the busier lifestyle back there?"

"Oh, no." Lavette found herself meeting his gaze before she thought. She looked away quickly. "I like the quiet here. It's so peaceful. Nobody rushes anywhere."

Josiah chuckled. "That's true. Around here, the summer heat teaches everyone to move slower to survive. Do you miss the green?"

Frowning, Lavette considered the difference from their lush surroundings in Virginia and the sparse growth of the desert. "This is different and takes some adjusting." She looked off at the mountains rising starkly against the sky. "There's a beauty here that can't be compared to my home. Everything seems bigger and wider, maybe grander." She stopped, embarrassed to have said so much.

"Sounds to me like you would enjoy living here. Why don't you plan to stay when Mrs. Sawyer goes back East? She can find someone else to work for her. I'm sure there are a lot of young women who would gladly accept a position."

"I can't do that." Lavette jumped up from her chair, her mending falling to the porch floor. Scrabbling to gather everything up, she wondered how this conversation had gotten so personal.

Josiah's shoulder brushed against hers. Lavette froze. He took her hand, turned it over, and placed her needle and thread in her palm, then closed her fingers over the implements. "I don't know why you can't do that, but I intend to find out."

Lavette fled into the house, letting the door slam shut behind her. She leaned back against the closed door, her whole body shaking. Why? Why did she have to meet this man now? Her life was set out before her, and she knew her place. She'd been comfortable with that until Mr. Washington entered the picture.

The sound of his heavy tread echoed on the boards of the porch. She held her breath, waiting for him to leave. As she began to relax, thinking he'd gone, the wooden entryway she rested against began to vibrate as he knocked.

Chapter 4

Amazement swept through Josiah as he watched the door slam shut behind Lavette. He still knelt on the rough boards of the porch, his hand tingling from the contact with hers. The warmth of her fingers lingered as if he still held them. Why had she rushed off like that? Had he said something he shouldn't have? Had he been too forward, inviting her to stay in Tucson when they'd only met today? He hadn't meant the invitation to sound so personal.

A deep sigh escaped him. She was as beautiful this evening as she'd been in the early morning light — maybe even more lovely, now that he'd had the chance to watch her. Although he enjoyed the glimpses of her cinnamon eyes, he loved watching those long eyelashes curl against her cheek. Since they'd begun to talk, he'd hardly been able to take his eyes from her long, slender fingers.

Helping her pick up her sewing supplies had been a gift from God because he'd wanted so much to touch her, to hold her hand.

Lord, You need to guide me. I don't know why she wants to run back East when she seems to like it here in Tucson. Help me to not be too pushy. I know she must be the one for me. Otherwise, You wouldn't have brought her by the shop right when I asked You about a wife. Now, please help me convince her that she's the one.

Standing up, Josiah noticed a basket of other mending pushed behind her chair. He grinned. All he had to do was ask and God answered. This was the opportunity he needed to see her again so soon. Maybe he could even understand why she'd run off like a scared rabbit. That frightened look in her eyes reminded him of an animal cornered by a hunter. No way did he want her to be afraid of him.

After picking up the basket, he strode across the porch. No sound came from inside the house. He wondered where she had gone, what she was doing and thinking. Taking a deep breath, he rapped his knuckles on the door, careful not to shake the old wood too much.

He waited. No tap of footsteps sounded. Where had she disappeared to so fast? Out the back door? Was she helping Mrs. Sawyer and didn't hear his knock? The door flung open, and he stepped back in startled surprise. Lavette faced him, still clutching the needle and thread with the skirt draped over her arm. Several more tight curls had pulled free from her bun and wound around her neck like a fine, wiry chain.

"Yes?" She sounded breathless, like she'd run a long distance. There hadn't been any footsteps, though. Realization made his grin widen. She'd been waiting on the other side of the door. Had she wanted to see him again?

"You left the basket on the porch." He held out the mending. She stared at it, seeming unsure whether she should reach out or not.

"Thank you, Mr. Washington." She grabbed the basket and stepped back into the house. "I have to go. I should check on Mrs. Sawyer."

As the door closed with a soft click, Josiah turned and sauntered off the porch. He pursed his lips and began to whistle the tune to the words running through his head.

There is a fountain filled with blood,
Drawn from Immanuel's veins
And sinners, plunged beneath that flood,
Lose all their guilty stains.

Ever since the night he'd heard that song at a revival meeting and later accepted Jesus, he'd felt the fountain hymn was his. Music often swirled through his head as he worked at the forge, the pounding of his hammer beating a rhythm while he whistled or sang a tune.

Taking in a deep draught of air, Josiah tried to sort out his tangled emotions. Lavette had to be the one the Lord sent for him. Hadn't she appeared right after his prayer this morning? Didn't she admit to liking Tucson and the slower paced lifestyle here? She wasn't someone enamored with big city life and the luxuries to be had back East.

So why did she insist she had to go back when Mrs. Sawyer left? Why did she run away when he mentioned her staying here? He could see from her reaction to his touch that she must feel something for him. "Why is she so afraid of me?"

"Probably because you're so mean looking."

Josiah jerked to a stop. He hadn't realized he'd spoken the words aloud. Quinn Kirby leaned against a building, his face red, trying his best not to laugh. Josiah drew his eyebrows together, attempting to look angry. "I don't recall asking your opinion."

"Then who were you asking?" Quinn let loose a long laugh and grasped his sides.

"Maybe the Lord and I were having a private discussion." Josiah bit back a grin.

Quinn clapped him on the shoulder. "Come on. I'm heading your direction. You can tell me all about why you think she's afraid of you. I'll be happy to give you any advice you need."

Josiah snorted. "As if you know it all." Shaking his head, he fell in beside Quinn, matching his longer stride to Quinn's shorter one.

"I'm gathering you went to see Miss Johnson, right?" The deputy gave Josiah an inquisitive glance.

"Yeah." Josiah waved his hand back toward the house where Lavette and Mrs. Sawyer were staying. An easy silence rested between the two men. In the past year, since Quinn had become a Christian, he often sought out Josiah to talk about a Scripture or a problem he needed advice on. Because of Conlon, Quinn often came to Josiah for scriptural advice. Sometimes the two commented on how he should have been a preacher with his understanding of the Bible and his love for Jesus. Because of his and Quinn's deepening friendship and the serious discussions they'd shared in the past, Josiah didn't hesitate to open up to him.

"You know this morning when I first met Miss Johnson?" At Quinn's affirmative, Josiah continued to relate the story of how God seemed to answer his prayer by sending Lavette at the precise moment Josiah asked for a wife.

Stopping beside the walkway to his house, Quinn turned to Josiah. "If you haven't eaten, why don't you join Kathleen and me for supper? She always fixes plenty of food, especially now that she isn't sick with the baby anymore."

Josiah chuckled. "I remember my mama being that way. She would be so sick for awhile, I thought sure she would die. The sickness used to scare me until my pa told me most women were that way when new babies were coming. After she got over the sickness though, she ate everything in sight."

"Lately all Kathleen does is eat and sleep." Quinn grinned. "I'll bet she thinks she does a lot more than that. In fact, I always have a tidy house, clean clothes, and a hot meal. She makes it look so easy, I think she's doing nothing."

The pair turned up the walkway. Many an evening, Quinn had invited Josiah to eat with him and Kathleen. Often Conlon and Glorianna Sullivan joined them. As much as Josiah loved his friends, he sometimes felt like he didn't belong. Tonight, however, he would enjoy talking with Kathleen and Quinn. Maybe they could help him make sense of these roiling feelings.

Leading the way around to the kitchen door, Quinn hesitated. Josiah took a deep breath. The air smelled of something burning. As Quinn reached to open the door, the portal flung open, and a billow of smoke engulfed them. Josiah coughed and blinked his stinging eyes.

"Kathleen?" Panic rang in Quinn's voice.

The smoke danced away on the breeze, and there stood Kathleen, tears streaming down her face, a smoking pot clutched in her cloth-covered hands. Quinn grabbed the cloths and the pan. Moving around Josiah, he set the smoking kettle on the ground. Standing next to Quinn, Josiah held his breath and peered down at what once might have been a piece of meat. The charred remains didn't look at all appetizing.

A long shuddering sob sounded behind them. Quinn and Josiah turned back to see Kathleen wiping her face with a handkerchief.

"Oh, Quinn, I'm so sorry." She covered her face with the hanky and turned her back on them.

"What happened?" Quinn moved up the steps and put his arm around his wife's shaking shoulders.

"I fell asleep again." The words came out in a wail. "I was so tired and thought if I could rest a few minutes, I'd be fine. I didn't even lay down in the bed, but sat in the chair in the living room. The next thing I knew, I was choking on smoke."

Quinn pulled her around into his embrace. "You know, this looks like a beautiful evening. Why don't we open the windows? Then we can stroll down to the Widow Arvizu's eatery with Josiah and have some supper." He brushed a strand of hair behind her ear. Watching Quinn wipe a tear from Kathleen's cheek, the tenderness of the moment gave Josiah an ache that settled in his heart. He longed so much for a woman to look at in the same way.

"You help Kathleen get ready, and I'll open the windows." Josiah clumped up the steps and past the couple before he succumbed to the emotion of the moment. He choked as the strong smell of burning meat and smoke hit him. He didn't want to think how close Kathleen had come to catching the house on fire. Although the walls were made of adobe and wouldn't burn readily, the contents would have caught fire.

By the time Kathleen washed and fixed her hair, fresh air had blown most of the heavy smoke from the house. Eyes puffy, Kathleen gave Josiah a watery smile. "I'm sorry about this, Josiah. I had a feeling you might be here for supper and planned to make plenty."

"I'll be proud to sit beside you at Arvizu's." Josiah knew Señora Arvizu's was the only place he was welcome to eat in the same room with the whites in town. "I'll even split the cost with Quinn. Of course, then I'll charge him extra on his next horseshoeing." He chuckled and Kathleen laughed.

Stepping through the door, Quinn held it open. Kathleen took his arm, and they all set off down the street. Stars twinkled overhead in a sky that seemed to go on forever. Josiah took a few deep breaths, careful not to let Kathleen notice. The smell of smoke lingered in his nostrils. His throat ached, and he wondered how Kathleen's felt.

"Did you know Josiah has a sweetheart?" Quinn's question jolted Josiah from his reverie.

"What?" Kathleen turned to look at Josiah. Her eyes sparkled in the light of the rising moon. "When did this happen?"

"He only met her today. She walked into his smithy, and he was smitten."

"Truly, Josiah? Tell me all about her."

Josiah groaned. His face warmed. "I'd rather talk about the fine weather we're having."

Kathleen sighed. "Now, Josiah, Quinn's the deputy. If you won't talk, I'll have him lock you up. Then you won't be able to escape my questions."

Quinn's laugh startled a dog at the side of the road. "You may as well give up. She'll keep after you until she knows every detail."

Shaking his head, Josiah heaved an exaggerated sigh. For the rest of the short walk to Arvizu's, he related once more the events of the day and his experience with Lavette. He could see Kathleen's excitement. He tried to keep the discouragement from his voice when he told her about Lavette leaving to go home soon. "How much longer did she say she would be here?"

"I don't recall if she said an exact time. I think she mentioned a few weeks." Josiah could see the light spilling out of the Arvizu eatery. His stomach protested the lack of food today. "I can't force her to stay. Maybe she has some reason to return to Virginia."

"Does she have a beau? She may be promised to someone already."

Reaching to open the door, Josiah shook his head. "How am I supposed to ask something like that?"

Kathleen swept through the door. She acted as if her burned dinner had been completely forgotten in the quest to solve his problems. Crossing the room to an empty table took a long time. Between Quinn and Kathleen, they knew everyone and stopped to chat several times. Josiah thought he might faint from hunger before they reached their destination. Waiting for Kathleen to be seated, he paid no attention to those around them or the few stares he received. He knew there were some who didn't accept his presence here. Only through the grace of God did others welcome him.

After Señora Arvizu explained all her problems, health and businesswise, to Kathleen and took their order, Kathleen turned to Josiah with a sweet smile on her face. "I know what you need, Josiah. You need someone to help you out with your cause. I'll get Glory, and we'll go to visit Mrs. Sawyer and Lavette."

"No." Talking ceased. People stared. Josiah shrank back onto the bench. He hadn't meant to be so loud. She'd surprised him. "I'll find a way to ask her."

"Nonsense." Kathleen patted his hand and winked at Quinn. "We'd heard there was someone new in that house. I've been meaning to wander over there for several days. Glory is always looking for a way to get out with the twins. She'll enjoy the walk."

Josiah knew he must have the look of doom on his face. Kathleen laughed.

"Don't you worry, Josiah. Glory could get a cactus to tell its life history. When she bats those lashes of hers, people fall all over themselves to tell her anything she wants. We'll find out all you need to know to court Lavette in a way she won't be able to resist."

Señora Arvizu placed steaming plates of food in front of them. The spicy scent made Josiah's stomach twist in anticipation. He bowed his head for a short prayer, then lifted his fork. How could he stop Kathleen and Glorianna? What if they said the wrong thing to Lavette and ruined his chances altogether?

"You may as well give up, Josiah." Quinn lifted a bite of beans to his mouth.

"What's that?" Josiah frowned, trying to decide what Quinn meant.

"Once Kathleen and Glorianna get something in their heads, stopping them is like standing in front of a locomotive with your hand out to halt the machine."

Kathleen smoothed a napkin in her lap. "I promise we'll be as discreet as possible. Before she knows what's happening, that girl will be dreaming of you all day long."

Quinn chuckled. "Maybe when we leave here, we can go to the telegraph office and send off for a preacher. We could even go to the mercantile and order the wedding gown."

Josiah hunched his shoulders, wishing he could disappear. Why had he ever talked about Lavette in the first place?

"I'd say you shouldn't consider your suit a sure thing."

The nasal voice behind him struck a chill down Josiah's back. He could see the stillness in Quinn's face and the dislike Kathleen tried to hide. Placing his fork on his plate, he turned to face Bertrand Mead.

"I don't know what you have to say about anything." Quinn spoke before Josiah had a chance.

The false smile on Mead's face turned Josiah's stomach. Pale, narrow eyes, filled with arrogance, looked down at him. "The girl will be mine. I happened to hear her singing this afternoon. She's incredible. When I've had the chance to talk to her, I'm sure she'll be willing to come and work for me. With a good voice and her looks, she won't want for opportunity." He gave a mirthless laugh. "I'm sure the men of this town will enjoy her immensely."

Chapter 5

Bile wormed its way up Josiah's throat, although he barely noticed the burning. His hands clenched into fists. Pushing against the table, he started to rise. Quinn clamped his hand over Josiah's. Their eyes met, and Josiah could read Quinn's message. Even though he wanted to ignore his friend, Mead wasn't worth a night or more in jail. This wasn't the South, but even so, blacks didn't have the freedom others did. For him to strike a white man would bring certain disaster upon himself and would affect those who stood by him.

Easing back onto the bench, Josiah forced his hands to relax. He pulled in a deep breath, praying as he did so.

"Mr. Mead, perhaps Miss Johnson will prefer to sing for our evangelist meetings when we have a preacher in town." Kathleen's voice carried a little too much sugar.

Josiah knew she was trying to help him.

Mead stepped to the side. Josiah could see him from the corner of his eye. The man settled his hat on his head as if making a fashion statement. Putting his walking stick under his arm, Mead nodded in Kathleen's direction. "Perhaps that's true, Mrs. Kirby. I'll go by tomorrow and discuss this with the lady in question." He straightened his coat. "However, it's been my experience that a lucrative offer such as I plan to give Miss Johnson will usually be too tempting to refuse."

Anger burned through Josiah as he watched the dandy stride from the restaurant. He felt so helpless to stop him. What Mead planned for Miss Johnson shouldn't be done to any woman. Taking advantage because she was a servant was despicable.

"Josiah, ease up." Quinn spoke low, but with a firmness that caught Josiah's attention. "If Miss Johnson is a respectable person, she'll turn him down no matter how lucrative his offer is. If she's the woman God has for you, then she's a decent person."

The swell of noise from the chattering diners wrapped around Josiah once more. He didn't know if they'd all quit talking or if he'd been so focused on Mead that he'd

61

shut out everything else. For a moment, he wondered how so many people could be going about their business like nothing had happened when he'd been so shaken.

A soft touch on his hand startled Josiah. He looked down to see Kathleen's small hand covering his larger one. Lifting his gaze to meet hers, he knew she hurt with him.

"Josiah, if this were Quinn or Conlon, what would you tell them to do?" Kathleen's soft words were almost lost in the cacophony around them.

Letting out the deep breath he hadn't realized he held, Josiah gave a tired smile. "I'd tell them to pray."

Kathleen smiled and patted his hand. "And I'll bet your mama would have said to finish your supper. Then you can go home and spend time in prayer. God knew this would happen, and you'll have to trust His plan even when you can't see it." She picked up a forkful of beans. "Tomorrow I'll get Glory, and we'll go by to visit Miss Johnson. You come for supper tomorrow night, and I'll tell you what we find out. This young lady won't be able to resist your charms with all of us praying for her and praising you."

Quinn shook his head. "I don't know

who to feel sorrier for, Josiah or Miss Johnson."

Smiling, Josiah picked up his fork, *Thank You, Lord, for friends like these. Please protect Lavette from Mead. You know he's up to no good.* The rest of the meal flew by. Between Quinn's stories of his day's adventures and Kathleen's tales of the Sullivan twins' escapades, Josiah didn't realize he'd finished his food until he looked down to find his plate clean. Standing, he thanked his friends and excused himself. He wanted to get home, spend some time with Jesus, and maybe even dream a little about expressive cinnamon eyes and wiry curls around a heart-shaped face.

"My Father, how long, my Father, how long, my Father, how long, poor sinner suffer here?" Lavette's heart ached as she sang. When she closed her eyes, she could still see the line of slaves marching to the fields, shoulders stooped from years of bending over plants, their voices lifting up this sad song. So many times, she'd felt guilty that her physical burden was lighter than theirs. She didn't have to suffer the hard labor they did. As she grew older and garnered the attention of Miss Susannah's father, Lavette often wished for the chance to be a slave in the fields, rather than one in the house.

Sprinkling the bread dough with a little more flour, Lavette folded and pushed the mass as if this were someone she had a grudge against. She tried to recall her mother's face or voice, but only a vague idea came to mind. She couldn't clearly see her family's faces anymore. Once in awhile, she could hear her mother's voice, but those times were getting fewer as the days went by. Oh, how she missed them all.

A light knock rattled the kitchen door. Shaking the excess flour from her hands, Lavette wiped the rest on her apron. Wishing she could check her hair but having no time, she crossed to open the door. Two young women stood on the porch. One of them had red hair, the other had a star-shaped birthmark on her cheek. Each held a young child on her hip.

"May I help you?" Lavette smoothed her floury apron.

"Hello." The dark-haired woman held out a luscious-looking cake. "I'm Kathleen Kirby, and this is my cousin, Glorianna Sullivan. We heard someone had moved into this house and thought we'd drop by to say hello."

"Thank you. My mistress is sleeping right now. I don't know when she'll be ready to receive callers. She hasn't been feeling well for some time." Lavette stared at the ground. One glance told her she didn't deserve to look at these women. They might be like Miss Susannah.

"Maybe we could come in and visit with you for awhile. Then, if your mistress is still asleep, we'll come by another time."

Not knowing what else to do, Lavette opened the door. As Glorianna stepped past Lavette, the little boy in her arms leaned back until his face was under Lavette's. He chortled, reaching his pudgy hands toward her. Bright blue eyes, full of mischief, stared at her.

"Andrew, come back here."

The boy disappeared from sight as the woman pulled him upright. Lavette chanced a glance at the other baby. The little girl had a thumb in her mouth, her wide green eyes taking in everything in the house. Red hair, a shade lighter than the other woman's, surrounded her head in a halo of curls.

"Oh, you have fixed this little place up so nice." Kathleen turned so Lavette could no longer see the baby, only the woman's back. "Are you making some bread?"

"Yes, Ma'am." Lavette followed the two women into the kitchen where her unfinished bread dough waited for more kneading. If she didn't get back to it soon, the whole batch would be ruined.

"You go right ahead and finish." Kathleen seemed to read Lavette's mind. "We don't want you to have to start over with this."

"Do you mind if we put the twins down?" Glorianna's question caught Lavette off guard.

"No, Ma'am. They won't hurt anything." Lavette watched as the twins were put on the floor. Andrew began to take hesitant steps across the room, stopping to give his mother a toothy grin. The little girl plopped down on her padded bottom, one hand twined in Kathleen's skirt as she examined the room from there. Lavette began to knead the bread, feeling a little uncomfortable. Should she go in and wake Mrs. Sawyer to let her know the ladies were here? Mrs. Sawyer was gaining strength, but Lavette didn't want to tire her.

"Mrs. Sawyer needs a lot of rest. She takes several naps during the day. Would you like me to wake her?" Lavette squeezed the bread, hoping to keep her hands from shaking. She never felt right around white folks she didn't know, and she hated the way she couldn't seem to stop from chattering. "Would you like to wait in the parlor where the chairs are nicer? We're only here for a short time, so the house isn't very fancy."

"We heard about you visiting Gretta and Paul. My husband is the lieutenant over Paul at Fort Lowell." Glorianna had a smile in her voice. "We do want to visit with your mistress, but we also wanted to call on you."

Lavette's hand stilled. Her gaze flitted up, catching both women looking at her. She dropped her gaze and continued to work the dough. "I'm not sure why you want to see me. I didn't do nothing wrong."

"Miss Johnson, we heard about you from a friend. He told us so much about you, we had to come and meet you for ourselves."

Lavette paused, trying to think who would be talking about her. "I don't know anyone here."

"You met Josiah Washington at the blacksmith shop yesterday. He speaks very highly of you."

Andrew toddled over to Lavette and wrapped his arms around her leg. Her skirt bunched up as he leaned against her, giving her the same charming grin he'd given Glorianna. She smiled and winked at him. He rested his head on her leg and stuck a finger in his mouth.

"I met Mr. Washington." Lavette didn't know what to say. She didn't want to admit that she'd been thinking of the man all day. Last night she'd had trouble falling asleep remembering the warm smile he'd given her as he left the house. She'd never heard of a black man being friends with whites. How could this be?

"Josiah is a wonderful man, don't you think?" Glorianna seemed to be the one doing all the talking. "He sure is taken with you."

Glorianna's comment sent a rush of pleasure spiraling through Lavette. Did Josiah think about her as much as she thought about him? He must be considering her some, to have told his friends about her.

"He seems like a very nice man, but I won't be here long enough to get to know him well. My time is taken with caring for Mrs. Sawyer."

"Josiah said you like the desert." Kathleen spoke up, and Lavette wondered at the change in subject.

"Oh, I do." She couldn't keep the enthusiasm from her voice. "I've heard the weather is very hot in the summer, but I'd rather face the heat than the ice and snow of the East. I grew up in the South and have never adjusted to the colder climate."

"So why don't you stay here when Mrs. Sawyer returns home?" Glorianna sounded pleased about the chance to ask the same question Josiah had asked. "Do you have someone special waiting for you?"

Anger swept through Lavette. How could these women understand her reasons? Had they ever belonged to anyone as a slave? Well, she had, and so had her family. In fact, she still belonged to someone. Freedom was something she would never experience, no matter how many wars were fought.

Smoothing the dough, Lavette covered the mass with a towel to let it rise. Stepping to one side, she waited for Andrew to let go of her skirt so she could move to the wash basin. She washed her hands, drying them on her apron. "I'll go see if Mrs. Sawyer is awake yet. If you ladies will follow me, I'll show you into the parlor where you can wait for her." Lavette knew her tone held a chill that would leave Glorianna and Kathleen wondering what had upset her, but she couldn't talk to them. They wouldn't understand.

No white person would.

Wriggling her shoulders, Lavette arched her back to ease the ache as she settled into the porch chair, her basket of mending beside her. She'd finished giving Mrs. Sawyer a bath and getting her to bed. The work today had exhausted her. All the lifting was taking a toll on her strength. Not only that, but the tension of the last two days and the lack of sleep last night added to her distress.

Pulling a nightgown from the pile of clothing that needed to be repaired, Lavette broke off a length of thread. Soon she would have to go to the mercantile to get more sewing supplies. The constant lifting and moving of her mistress proved to be hard on the clothes, both hers and Mrs. Sawyer's. Her needle wove in and out, repairing the tear as her thoughts strayed to last night on this same porch.

She could almost feel Josiah standing by the railing near her chair. He had such magnetism, it seemed to linger long after he left. The thought of his wide grin and deep voice set her heart fluttering. She stopped sewing a moment to fan her face.

Never had a man affected her like this. Perhaps she should encourage Mrs. Sawyer to return east early so she could get away from Josiah's influence before she lost her heart to him. Surely that hadn't happened yet. How could she have fallen for him in such a short time? Inside, a small voice let her know that even if she left the man now, he'd already changed her life. She would never forget him.

"Evenin', Miss Johnson."

Lavette jumped. The needle slid smoothly into her thumb. "Ouch." She jerked her thumb away, nursing the small wound. The man she'd run from at Josiah's blacksmith shop yesterday stood in front of her, his hat tilted at a rakish angle. A black stick cane with a carved silver head stuck out from under his arm. Lifting his hat, he nodded at her.

She clutched the sewing to her breast, wanting to run. Since he stood between her and the door, there was no escape this time. The feral gleam in his eyes reminded her of Miss Susannah's father. That's why she'd fled yesterday and that's why fear paralyzed her today.

"I thought we could talk for a few minutes." He leaned closer. She could smell the cloying scent of some lotion.

"I got to get back inside."

"But you just came out here." His lips tilted in a lascivious smile. "Why don't you relax? I won't hurt you."

"What do you want?" Nausea burned Lavette's throat.

"Why, I only want to make you an offer, Miss Johnson. Nothing more." He took a step closer. She backed farther into the chair.

"I'm not interested." She grabbed up her basket of sewing without taking her eyes from Mead.

"But you haven't heard my offer." He chuckled, a menacing sound that reminded her of the way a snake petrified its victims to catch them. "I heard you yesterday. I'd like for you to come and sing in my establishments. You will earn a good wage and have people wait on you for a change. That's not a bad offer, is it?"

She stood so fast, the chair tipped back with a crash. "I can't do that." She eased past him to the door. "Leave me alone. I can't work for you."

"Oh, but I think you can, Miss Johnson." His hand closed on her arm, and a foreboding chill raced through her. "You see, I've found out things about you already. I know the reason you're here with your mis-

tress, and I know how to make you mine."
Releasing her arm, he swiveled around and
stepped off the porch. Whistling a jaunty
tune, he ambled down the path to the
street, leaving Lavette shaking with terror
that he would be able to carry through on
his threat.

Chapter 6

Two days had passed since Josiah had visited Lavette. He hadn't been able to stay away any longer. The excitement of seeing her again made him feel like a little boy with a secret so big, he couldn't stay still with wanting to tell someone. He wanted to run and shout with the sensation. The grin on his face must be showing everyone he passed exactly what he was thinking and feeling.

The bag dangling from his hand rattled with his movement. He glanced down, hoping this offering would make Lavette more receptive to him. Maybe she wouldn't run away this time. Perhaps they could sit down together, and he would find out why she feared getting to know him. He knew this was too soon to consider touching those slender hands of hers, but the thought made his heart race anyway.

Last night Josiah ate supper with the

Kirbys and the Sullivans. The resulting conversation proved very enlightening. Glorianna and Kathleen told him all about their conversation with Lavette, but the best part came from Conlon and the talk he had with Paul Ashton about his mother-in-law and her servant. Paul said Lavette had no beau waiting that he knew about.

Whistling his favorite hymn, Josiah turned up the path that led to the Sawyer house. He wiped his damp palms on his pants, glad he'd taken the time to bathe and change before coming over here. Working a forge wasn't the cleanest job, but it was honest labor. Josiah could remember all the times he worked alongside his father, learning about horses and shoeing. He'd never regretted learning the blacksmith trade.

Tapping softly on the door, Josiah waited. He didn't want to wake Mrs. Sawyer if she was resting. No one answered, and he couldn't hear any movement from inside. He knocked a little louder, then tilted his head to one side listening. From somewhere he could hear the sound of an angel singing. The music drifted in and out on the breeze, tantalizing the senses and leaving him wanting to hear more.

Stepping off the porch, Josiah walked

around the corner of the house. The singing got louder, although it still seemed faint. The angel must not want anyone to hear. At the back of the house he halted, amazed at the vision that greeted him.

Lavette stood with her back to him, pulling laundry from a clothesline. As she folded a heavy sheet, a soft melody issued from her — a slow, sad tune about suffering. The song made him want to weep and beg for more at the same time. Her voice brought to mind butterflies in the summer sun or birds soaring in the heavens. Never in his life had he heard anything more beautiful.

The tune and the words were simple enough. Josiah didn't know how long he stood there before he found himself humming along. As Lavette started on another verse, he caught the idea and joined his bass to her lovely voice. He couldn't have stopped himself if he tried. The music seemed to be drawn out on its own free will without asking his permission. For a moment, their voices blended in a beautiful harmony as if God created them for this express purpose. Lavette stopped midnote. She whirled around. The nightgown in her hand almost dropped to the dirt.

A silly grin stretched Josiah's cheeks. He

could stand here all day watching her. Lavette was taller than most women, although she was still several inches shorter than he. Lithe and willowy, she moved with the grace of one of those ballerinas he'd seen when he lived back East as a boy. Of course, he'd never seen them dance, but he remembered the time he and his father were driving Mr. Bellingham somewhere. Those dancers seemed to flow.

"Whatever are yah doin' heah?" Lavette's Southern accent seemed more pronounced now, when she was upset.

"I didn't mean to scare you." A clink from the bag at his side reminded Josiah of his excuse. He lifted the bag in the air. "I brought you some things I thought might be useful."

She stared at him, suspicion appearing to make her cautious. After folding the nightgown, she placed it in the basket at her feet. "I don't recall us needing anything."

"The other night you mentioned wanting another knife. You didn't give me the one you wanted repaired, so I brought a couple of new ones for you. Cooking can be a mite difficult when you only have one." He reached into the bag and pulled out a poker. "I also brought some utensils and tools I thought you might use. Since you're only here for a short time, I thought maybe you wouldn't have all you needed. You can return them before you go home." His heart clenched as he added the last.

Brushing a mass of curls from her forehead, Lavette reached for the last piece of clothing on the line. The wayward curls landed back on her brow before she had time to lift her hand away. They gave her a sweet look that somehow reminded him of his own mother when she worked with her hair frizzing in mad disarray.

Slinging the bag of utensils over his shoulder, Josiah hurried after Lavette as she carried the full basket to the house. He stretched out a hand to open the door for her. Lavette turned to him, her mouth open like she planned to invite him in. Her fingers closed around the latch, and his covered hers before he could stop. Lavette's eyes widened. Josiah couldn't breathe. Time seemed to stand still as they stood transfixed, gazing into one another's eyes.

Lavette moaned and tugged her hand from under his. Josiah pulled the latch and opened the door.

"Can I get the basket for you?"

She darted through the open door, her

gaze downcast. "No, thank you. I'll put the clothes in the other room and be right back. Please have a seat." Her skirt swished as she crossed the room.

Stepping inside, Josiah closed the door behind him. His hand still tingled from the contact with her. His arms ached with the desire to hold her close. Shaking his head, he put the bag of utensils on the table and began to examine the room. How could he feel this way about a woman so fast? Until a few days ago, he hadn't recognized the longing inside as loneliness and a suppressed desire for a wife. Was he reacting to Lavette simply because he'd finally admitted the truth to himself?

"May I offer y'all a drink?" Even her speaking voice carried a trace of the melodic singing he'd heard outside. "We have some cake from last night's supper too."

He grinned. "I believe you said the right words. I'm never one to pass on a piece of something sweet and a cup of water or coffee. Will you join me?" He waited while Lavette dished up two pieces of cake, a tiny one for herself and a huge one for him. His mouth watered, and his stomach growled.

The corner of her mouth turned up at the sound. "Sounds like you must be starving. Did you miss your lunch today?"

He chuckled. "If I haven't eaten in the last hour, my stomach thinks I'm dying of starvation."

"We can't have that, then." Lavette carried the plates to the table. Turning to the stove, she lifted the coffeepot, then brought two cups. "Do you want a little milk or sweetening in your coffee?"

"No, thank you, but you can leave the pot here. I'll probably need a refill." Josiah held the chair for Lavette, then sat across from her. He wasn't sure if he could take his eyes off of her long enough to eat, she was so beautiful.

"Mmm. This is delicious. Kathleen Kirby makes a cake exactly like this."

Lavette's mouth twitched. She began to giggle. Even her giggle didn't sound girlish, but musical. Josiah wanted to shake himself. He must have it bad, whatever this was.

"You seem to find that funny. Did you get the recipe from Kathleen? She told me she visited you yesterday." He stared as Lavette broke into peals of laughter. Tears streamed down her face. She pulled a handkerchief from her pocket and wiped her cheeks.

"I'm sorry." She gasped for a breath. "Mrs. Kirby brought the cake over yesterday when she and Mrs. Sullivan came to visit. I didn't mean to make you think I baked this. I'm not sure why I'm laughing."

Josiah began to chuckle. "I'm not either, but I'd rather see you laughing than throwing something at me."

"Like the cake?" She laughed harder.

"Like the cake." He grinned as he watched her struggle to control her mirth. This woman was as changeable as a cat he used to have. One day the beast would be friendly, the next, a tigress ready to attack. He'd loved the cat, though, because she was never boring. He thought life with Lavette would never be dull, either.

Giddiness welled up inside Lavette. She couldn't seem to stop laughing. *What is the matter with me?* Since the moment Josiah's fingers closed over hers on the door latch, she hadn't been able to think straight. *No, that's not true.* A small voice whispered the words in her mind. Since the moment she'd heard his deep bass blending with her voice, she'd lost the ability to think rationally. Something had snapped, and she thought it must be the protective covering she'd put over her heart long ago.

When his hand touched hers, she was transfixed. The look in his eyes mesmerized her. She found she wanted to have him hold her, to feel those strong arms around her lending strength and comfort. The sudden desire to belong to the man of her dreams had been almost more than she could bear.

Now, he was sitting here, trying to eat cake, and all she could do was cackle like some lovesick hen. That thought made her start laughing all over again. She could see Josiah strutting around like a rooster. No, he wasn't like that at all. He wouldn't think the world of himself, but he would think the world of his wife. If he strutted around, it would mean he was proud of her.

"You have the most beautiful soprano I ever heard." Josiah's words were like cold water and sobered her in an instant.

"Thank you." She ducked her head and began to cut a bite from her cake.

"I remember Mrs. Thompson back home. She had a fine voice. We would hear her every Sunday when she stood up and sang at church." Josiah's bright gaze caught hers when she looked up. "But Mrs. Thompson couldn't sing at all compared to you. You make me think the angels are listening so they can take lessons."

Fire burned in her cheeks. Miss Susannah's papa talked about how pretty her voice was, too. He even took her with him to a house where he wanted her to sing for the folks. She hated the memory. The women there hadn't been dressed right. The men were smoking and drinking. The talk made her ears burn, and she was sure God would never forgive her. Maybe He hadn't; look what all had happened to her. Miss Susannah's papa insisted that when Lavette grew up, that was all she'd be good for — to entertain and work in one of those places. For so long after the war, she'd been terrified to sing.

"Do you enjoy the music in church at your home?" Josiah must not be able to see the turmoil going on inside her. She thought it would be obvious for anyone to notice. "We don't have a regular church here." Josiah continued without noticing her distress. "Sometimes we get a pastor passing through, and he stays for a few weeks to preach to us, but mostly we get together with friends and share Scripture."

Lavette pushed away from the table and picked up her plate with the uneaten cake. Before walking to the washing tub, she scraped the cake into the scrap bucket. She knew what would happen when she told

Josiah about her beliefs. He'd be gone so fast, she wouldn't hear him leave. She could tell from looking at him, he was a decent man. He wouldn't want to be seen with the likes of her.

"Maybe this Sunday you could join me when I meet with the Sullivans, the Kirbys, and some others."

She gripped the edge of the washtub, willing her hands not to pick up the plate and throw it at him. Didn't he understand? Not only was she not worthy of him, she wasn't free to love him, either. She would never be free. Anger at that thought bubbled up like acid, eating through her.

"I don't go to church." She spat out the words.

"This isn't like church exactly." He stood and brought his empty plate and cup over to her. "We're friends, taking time to share some Bible and to pray. Afterwards, we eat the noon meal together. They're good people, and I'm sure you'll love them as much as I do."

Taking his dishes, she plunked them into the basin. Whirling around, she was startled to see he still stood there, a solid mountain of a man. She tilted her head back to look in his face. The anger drained away. How could this man affect her so?

Every fiber in her being was aware of him. He was like a magnet, drawing her to him, and she was helpless to resist.

"I have to take care of Mrs. Sawyer."

"I heard her daughter and son-in-law are taking her to their house for the day. That means you'll be here all by yourself, unless you have other friends in town that I don't know about." His grin softened, and he leaned closer.

Lavette wanted to move back, but the wash basin wouldn't allow that. "I don't go to church."

"You said that before, but this isn't going to church. This is friends getting together." His grin widened. "The only one of us that bites is little Andrew, and then only when he's getting another tooth."

She couldn't help herself. She chuckled. "I've met Andrew. He's adorable, and I don't think you're very nice to say mean things about him."

He pretended to be stricken. "Oh, I'm not being mean. I'm telling the honest truth. The last time he cut a tooth, I carried the evidence on my thumb for a week." He touched her arm, sending her emotions awry. "Will you come, please?"

"I don't even have a Bible." What a feeble excuse. *Maybe I should tell him I'll be sick by Sunday. After all, thinking of spending the day with all of them talking about God could make me ill.*

His huge hand touched her cheek. The warmth in his gaze stole her breath. When he spoke, his voice was husky with emotion. "That's no problem. I'll share mine."

Chapter 7

The door of the mercantile squeaked as Lavette pushed it open. A mixture of smells rushed out to greet her. The earthy scent of burlap, spices, leather, and an undefined musty odor all combined in an aroma that made identifying the more subtle fragrances difficult. High walls lined with shelves were packed full of assorted necessities. Her hand tightened on the short list she'd brought.

A group of men in the back of the store glanced up. Their stares made her want to fidget as the door creaked shut behind her. The brightness of the sun and the dim interior made distinguishing the men impossible, but she knew they'd stopped talking and watched her. Fear clutched at her with icy fingers. She wanted to fling the door open and run home as fast as she could.

Blinking, Lavette forced her feet to carry her to the counter, where a middle-aged man waited. His large mustache wiggled as he smiled at her. "May I help you?"

"I need some things." She tried to keep her voice from quaking but knew she hadn't succeeded. Holding out her trembling hand, she placed the crumpled list on the counter.

"Let's see." He frowned and put on a pair of spectacles. Squinting at the writing, he glanced up at her. "Thread, a pound of sugar, beans." He continued reading the list silently "I'll have these things ready in a few minutes, if you'd like to look around."

She shook her head. "Thank you. I'll wait here." She kept her gaze lowered, trying to keep from seeing what the men in the back of the room were doing. One of them let out a loud guffaw, followed by laughter from the rest. She glanced around for the clerk. He wasn't in sight.

Murmuring and snickering alternated from the group in the back. Lavette could feel a trickle of sweat inching down her back. Her muscles ached from staying still so long. Where was the man who took her order? Could she leave the cash on the counter and come back to pick up the goods later? She knew that wouldn't work. What if someone came along and took the coins before the man returned? Then, she would be in trouble with him and with Mrs. Sawyer for wasting money.

The ribaldry grew louder, along with a few comments that made her ears burn. Reaching into her bag, she fished around for the change Mrs. Sawyer had given her. She could hardly hear the jangling over the racket from the back of the store. Why hadn't she waited until tomorrow, when Mr. Ashton would be able to go to the mercantile for them?

From the corner of her eye, she saw one of the men sauntering in her direction. She froze, her fingers clenched so hard around the coins that they cut into her palm.

"Well, hello there, Miss Johnson. What a pleasure meeting you here." Bertrand Mead's nasal whine sent a chill racing down her spine. She shivered.

"I've been telling some of the boys here about you and how well you can sing. They were wondering if you would give us a little preview." Mead stopped next to her. She gagged on the nauseating scent of him. "I told them you would be entertaining in one of my establishments soon, and they are very excited. How about a song?"

"No." Her lips trembled. "Leave me alone."

Mead turned toward the men. "She's a little shy. Perhaps if you were to make it worth her while, she would give us a tune." His voice lowered. "She might even remember you favorably when you come to my place."

A chorus of hoots and laughter jolted Lavette. She jumped and began to sidle closer to the door. She didn't care about the items she came to buy. All she wanted was to get away from these men. Oh, why was the door so far away from her?

"Now, don't think you can run off, Miss Johnson." Mead took hold of her arm and began to drag her back to the table where the other men sat. Lavette couldn't look up. She didn't want to see the stares. Memories from her childhood haunted her, wrapping her in a cloak of terror.

"My, my, these gentlemen really do want to hear you, Miss Johnson." Mead pulled her to a stop beside the table. She could see a pile of coins thrown in the center. Mead's fingers held her in a painful grip. "Let's hear you do something for the men." His grip tightened, and she feared he might break her arm.

"Well, if you won't sing for us, let's at least let them get a look at your pretty face. I'm sure these men will want to look you up when you belong to me." Mead clasped her jaw and forced her head up. She closed her eyes, wishing the ground would open and swallow her.

"Here you are, Miss." The clerk swept through a curtained-off area at the back of the store. "I'm sorry I took so long. We were out of the thread you needed, and I had to find the new shipment in the back. Will this be all?"

Mead released her as the clerk swept past them, his arms full of packages. Lavette ran after him in her haste to get away from Mead and his cronies. Her heart pounded. Her hands shook so badly she dropped the money she pulled from her reticule. Scrambling on the floor, she did her best to retrieve it all. Laughter rang from the table at the back of the mercantile.

"Thank you." Lavette managed to get the words out as the clerk finished wrapping her purchases together in a paper and tying them with a string. She could feel Mead's gaze on her. What if he followed her? What could she do?

Stepping outside, Lavette reveled in the warmth of the sun. Her body felt chilled, as if she'd been exposed to the worst winter storm imaginable. Starting off down the street, she wanted to run but knew that was foolish. Mead was probably laughing about her with his friends. She'd been someone they made fun of, not someone he was truly serious about.

A door creaked behind her. Her heart pounded. Stomach churning, she glanced over her shoulder. Bertrand Mead stood outside the mercantile, watching her. With a deliberate smile, he began to stalk after her. Feeling like a rabbit running from a fox, Lavette quickened her pace.

She could not get to the house before he caught up with her. Mead's legs were longer. Even if she could run that far, he could easily outdistance her. She had no defense against him.

Hurrying around the corner, Lavette began to trot. Her skirts caught at her legs, slowing her down, threatening to trip her. Heavy footsteps sounded from behind. A cruel snigger let her know what Mead thought of her efforts to elude him. A sob tore through her chest. *Help me.* She wanted to scream the words aloud, but couldn't get them out.

Please, someone help me. No one paid attention to her. Some even pointedly ignored what was happening.

The footsteps were closer. Mead would

have her in a moment. She picked up her skirts and raced full tilt around a corner. The wall she ran into wasn't brick. For a moment she didn't realize she'd run into a person. Only when arms came around her, did she understand. One of Mead's men must have gone out a back way to catch her. How stupid she'd been to fall into such a trap.

Lavette twisted and fought to no avail. The package of goods she'd bought fell to the ground. The arms holding her felt like iron. He spoke, but she refused to listen. This man might be stronger than she, but she would at least put up a fight before they dragged her away.

"She doesn't seem to want you, Blacksmith." Mead's whine cut through her fear. Lavette stilled.

"I'm taking her home, Mead. She doesn't want to go with you." Josiah's deep voice rumbled in his chest. Lavette's ear pressed tight against him.

Josiah. He would protect her. She quit struggling and rested against him, so exhausted, she knew if he let go she would fall. He smelled of horses, smoke, and sweat, reminding her of her father and comfort. She wanted to stay there forever, to hide from the evil of the world.

"You all right?" Josiah's question spoken close to her ear sent a shiver down her spine, a very different kind of shiver from the one she got when Mead spoke to her.

She nodded. He seemed to understand, for his arms tightened a moment, then eased their hold.

"Let go of the girl." Anger gave Mead's voice a shrill sound. "I'll take her home. I need to talk to her owner, anyway."

Josiah stiffened. "No one is her owner. She's employed by Mrs. Sawyer. We aren't slaves anymore, Mead, no matter how much you want us to be."

Lavette tensed. Not slaves anymore? Was he blind? Didn't he understand they would always be in bondage? She started to push away, but Josiah's arms tightened, holding her close.

"Oh, I know they fought a war for emancipation, but this girl still belongs to the lady. She'll be for sale, and I'm going to buy her. If you don't believe me, ask her. For now, you can have her, but she'll be mine soon enough, and you won't get near her."

Lavette could hear Mead's heavy steps fading as he returned the way he had come. Fear tore through her. What if Mrs. Sawyer agreed to let Mead have her?

94

Money could buy most anything. Hadn't she seen that, growing up on Wild Oak plantation?

"I have to get home. Thank you." Lavette pushed back, and this time Josiah let go of her. She stepped away, unable to look at him. Her foot bumped against the package from the mercantile. Picking it up, she hugged the goods to her, wishing she were back in Josiah's arms.

"What did he mean? Why does he think you're still a slave?" Josiah stood like a mountain in front of her.

"Mrs. Sawyer will be expecting me. I need to get back to her." Lavette eased to one side.

"Wait." Josiah's command halted her. His huge fingers cupped her face, lifting until she looked at him. "We have to talk. Maybe now isn't the time. I'll come by this evening after you put your mistress to bed. We can discuss this on the porch."

She could see the compassion in his eyes. His touch warmed her, banishing thoughts of Mead and his associates. Tears clogged her throat. She blinked and nodded. Telling her story was too painful, but for some reason, she felt confiding in Josiah would help. Maybe he would understand why they had no future. Before she

95

came to care for him more than she already did, she should tell him the truth. Then he would leave and never see her again.

Josiah stopped in the shadow of a paloverde tree as he turned onto the path leading up to Lavette's house. He could see her seated on the porch, her head bent over her mending. Clenching his fists, he recalled the fright in her eyes when she barreled into him while being chased by Bertrand Mead. At the time, he hadn't known what he wanted more — to beat Mead to pulp or to hold and protect Lavette. In the end, common sense won. Although she fought like a tiger at first, his arms well remembered the feel of her trembling against him once she'd realized who held her.

After Mead left and she'd calmed down, he'd walked her home. Lavette insisted he didn't have to do that, but he wouldn't have trusted Mead not to sneak around and meet up with her. Of course, he hadn't suggested that to Lavette. He wouldn't want to scare the poor girl more than she already was.

He admired her spirit. As he'd pointed out to his friends, she'd been born a slave, and that's all she'd known until the war ended. Having been raised in the North by parents who'd been set free, Josiah had never been a slave, but he'd heard plenty of stories. Even as a child, a beautiful girl like Lavette would have caught the attention of the male owners of the plantation. He gritted his teeth. What had she endured that made her so afraid?

All afternoon, as he worked, Josiah hadn't been able to banish the thoughts of Mead and his words about Lavette belonging to Mrs. Sawyer. How could that be? He'd tried to think of every way he could imagine, but nothing made sense. There were no more slaves in the States, and that's where Mrs. Sawyer and Lavette came from.

Lavette glanced up from her sewing and started when she noticed him. Josiah strode forward, not wanting her to think him someone else in the fading light. If all she saw was the outlined figure of a man, she could easily mistake him for someone who would frighten her. That would never do.

"Good evening, Miss Johnson." The boards of the porch creaked under his weight.

"Evenin'." Lavette seemed to huddle

deeper into the chair, her hands clutching the mending against her breast. She appeared to want to run rather than talk to him.

Walking quietly to avoid bothering Mrs. Sawyer, Josiah was surprised to see a second chair waiting beside the vine-covered trellis on the other side of Lavette. She must have brought the chair out after he'd walked her home today. Josiah couldn't hide the grin of satisfaction in knowing she might have looked forward to seeing him at least a little. He sank into the chair and faced her, drinking in her beauty before the light faded. He knew he would never tire of watching Lavette Johnson.

"Did you have a lot of work today?" Her soft, Southern accent thrilled him. She picked at the loose thread on the garment in her lap.

"This afternoon I went out to the fort again to do some more horses for Conlon. I fixed a buggy wheel for Doc Meyer and did a few other odd jobs." Josiah eased to one side of the chair to avoid a knot in the wood that poked his back. He didn't want to make small talk. He wanted answers to his questions, but now that he was here, he hesitated to force Lavette to talk. She seemed so frightened, and he didn't know why.

"Have you eaten? I could fix you something, or we have some dried apple pie if you'd like a piece."

"I already ate, but I never turn down apple pie." Josiah's mouth began to water at the thought.

Lavette jumped up. The thread clattered to the porch floor and rolled to a stop by Josiah's boot. They both reached for the spool at the same time. Lavette's slender fingers closed over Josiah's. She glanced up, her eyes wide. Jerking away, she straightened. Josiah picked up the thread and handed it to her.

Holding tight to the spool, Josiah caught Lavette's hand as she reached out. "I'd love a piece of your pie, but this won't keep me from asking what I want to know. Why does Mead think he can own you? The war ended nine years ago. Slaves were set free. I want to know why you're so afraid he'll get control over you."

Lavette tugged her hand free. "I don't care if the war is over. I'll never be liberated. I'm still in bondage and always will be." She turned and rushed into the house, letting the door slam behind her.

Chapter 8

Lavette's hands shook as she lifted the generous slice of pie from the tin. How could she have acted that way toward Josiah? He only wanted to help her. He cared, while most people in her life didn't. She blinked back tears as she poured a cup of coffee. This was the reason she hadn't wanted to get to know Josiah. She didn't want to lose her heart to a man she couldn't marry. She picked up the pie and coffee, trying to keep from sloshing the liquid. Was she too late? Had she already lost her heart to this gentle giant?

The evening breeze carried a welcome hint of cool, wiping the traces of tears from Lavette's eyes as she stepped through the door. Josiah still sat in the chair, bent forward, his arms resting on his knees. Head bowed, he looked as though he were praying, although not a sound issued from him. Lavette recalled the times her papa and mama prayed together. They hadn't been quiet.

The porch creaked. Josiah raised his head. The anguish in his eyes tore at her heart. She longed to tell him everything would work out fine. She'd been in servitude most of her life and adjusted to the idea. Most of the time, belonging to someone else didn't bother her. The only time she'd lived differently had been a miserable period in her life. Remaining enslaved had been her choice, a decision she rarely regretted as she recalled the good her sacrifice had done for her mother.

"Here's your pie, and I brought you a cup of coffee." His fingers brushed against hers as he accepted the plate and cup. Lavette couldn't help the tremor of delight that raced up her arm.

"Thank you." Josiah set the mug on the porch beside his chair. He leaned back and placed the pie on his massive leg as if the appendage were a table. He left the sweet untouched as he crossed his arms over his chest.

"I'd like to hear why you think you're still a slave. I can understand it would be hard to discuss, but we need to talk."

"Why?"

"Because I care what happens to you. I don't want you to be afraid every time you walk down the street, thinking you might end up belonging to someone like Mead."

Lavette shuddered. She rubbed her arms. She couldn't look at Josiah, but stared at the black gleam of his coffee. "I can't tell you without relating how this happened. It'll take too long."

"I've got time." Josiah rested his ankle on top of his knee, leaning back farther into the chair. He picked up the pie and cut a bite, chewing like he had forever to sit on this porch. "Why don't you start by telling me about your family."

"My mama and papa were slaves on the Wild Oaks plantation in Alabama. I was born about the same time as Miss Susannah, the owner's daughter. Since we were the same age, I became her playmate. She had four older brothers, but no sisters." Lavette twisted her fingers together in her lap.

"Some people thought I had it easy because I didn't have to work in the fields." Terror rose up like bile in her throat. "I can't tell you how many times I wanted to be in the fields and away from the horrors of the house."

She glanced up to see Josiah holding the still-unfinished pie. His look held compassion and knowing. He'd probably heard the tales of what happened to girl slaves when they were at the mercy of their masters' whims. She rubbed her arms again, hoping he would think the evening air caused the chill.

"Did you get to stay with your folks? I know a lot of children were separated from their families."

"I think I was kept at the plantation because of being Miss Susannah's playmate. My two older brothers and one older sister were sold off before they were half-grown. That like to broke my mama's heart."

"Did you find them after the war?" She could hear the anguish Josiah was trying to hold back.

"My papa tried to find them, but he couldn't. I have a younger brother and two younger sisters. Papa didn't have much time to go off looking for the lost ones when he also had to feed all of us."

"Where are your parents now?"

Feeling cool air on her cheeks, Lavette reached up to wipe away the tears with the back of her hand. "Alabama. Papa's job at Wild Oaks was in the stables. He has a knack for working with horses." She drew a shaky breath.

"At the end of the war, Papa worked hard to provide for us. Mama grew a garden, and Papa found what jobs he could. Out in the country, there weren't many. Most of the plantation owners were ruined. No one could afford to hire Papa or Toby, my brother, to work for them very often. Papa finally found a job on a big farm. It wasn't much different than being a slave. The landowner didn't pay enough, but he allowed us to get what we needed from his store on credit. Papa tried hard to keep from doing that. He didn't want to be indebted to anyone. We were barely gettin' by when Mama had the accident."

Lavette stared down at the mending in her lap. Josiah's hands engulfed hers, warming them, offering her comfort. She had no idea when he'd moved closer.

"What happened?"

"We were in town getting a few things. I had to watch Lila and little Nellie while Mama crossed the street to get to the tanner's. Mama stepped into the street to come back over just as a man in a buggy whipped around the corner." Lavette's throat closed. The memory filled her with horror all over again.

"Did she get trampled?"

Lavette shook her head. "No, the buggy tilted, catching my mama and throwing her to one side like a rag doll." Her voice dropped to a whisper. "I can still see the look of horror on her face. I can hear the driver yell as he jumped away, hitting his head against a watering trough. The horses' ears were laid back, its eyes wild. My mama didn't have a chance."

Pulling a hand free, Lavette covered her mouth. "We heard later the driver died. The doctor said Mama was lucky to have been hit by the wagon instead of being run over. She had a broken arm, some broken ribs, and bruises, but she was unconscious for days. We didn't think she would ever wake up. When she did, she couldn't recall what happened. Sometimes I didn't think she really remembered us.

"For a long time, Papa couldn't work enough to feed us. I tried to find food in the woods. A few others tried to help us, but most people we knew were as bad off as we were. There were many nights when the baby, Nellie, would cry herself to sleep because she was so hungry. I thought we would all starve. Papa couldn't let that go on, so he began to borrow from the store. We got deeper and deeper in debt."

Josiah's callused hands rubbed hers with a gentle, soothing motion. His quiet strength seemed to give her enough courage to continue.

"One day, Michael Sawyer came to see us. We'd almost given up hope. Food was so scarce, I didn't know what we would eat the next day." Lavette drew in a shaky breath. "It turned out that Mr. Sawyer's son-in-law was responsible for the accident. When he heard what happened, Mr. Sawyer felt beholden to find us and try to make things right. The problem was, he didn't have much after the war, either. While he was talking to Papa, I came home from foraging in the woods. He said he had an idea and told Papa he would return the next day."

For several minutes, Lavette sat in silence, unable to continue. Josiah's thumb rubbed the palm of her hand. "What did he do?"

"He said his mother needed someone to work for her. His mother, Mrs. Sawyer, had some health problems. The doctors thought she would improve if she moved north to get away from the damp air. Her brother up North would help her, but she needed someone to go along to care for her."

"Lavette, being a servant isn't at all like being a slave. You're free to quit and find work somewhere else."

"That's what her son feared. To keep me

106

from quitting and leaving her alone, he offered me a contract similar to an indentured servant's. He would give my father enough money to pay off his debt. Papa would be able to move to the city, where he could find better work. In fact, Mr. Sawyer had a friend in the city looking for a good man to take charge of his livery. He promised medical help for Mama, too." She drew in a shaky breath. "He also said I would earn a small monthly wage."

"What did your father do?"

"He turned him down. He said he'd watched three of his children be sold off, and he wouldn't sell his own daughter, not for any amount of money. Mr. Sawyer said he would give us some time to think about it and would return in a couple of days."

Josiah's knees brushed hers. He leaned forward, his body and his face betraying his tension.

"Mama still wasn't strong. The girls were old enough to start helping out, though. I couldn't let Papa turn down such a generous offer. I waited until everyone except the two of us was sleeping. Then I told him that I chose to become Mrs. Sawyer's servant. That way he wouldn't be selling me off. I would be offering my services. I begged him to let me do this for him and Mama. They could go to the city and get a better job. Maybe Mama could even get some help for the headaches she continued to have."

"But you couldn't have been very old." Josiah cleared his throat and blinked.

"I wasn't too old, only seventeen. Living as a slave, a person grows up fast. Some girls were married by that age. I'd been caring for my brother and sisters for a long time. Since Mama had been sick, I'd pretty much run the house." She didn't object when Josiah rested his forehead against their joined hands.

"When Mr. Sawyer came back, I told him I'd take care of his mama, but I couldn't do it until my family had paid their debts and moved to the city. He gave Papa the money right away and gave us the address of a man he knew who wanted to hire Papa. It didn't take long to pack up the meager belongings we had. Within a few days, I was a slave once more." She shrugged and gave a small smile. "Oh, I know this is a little different, I had a choice, but still I'm not free to decide what I want to do."

"How much longer is left on your contract?"

"I signed the contract for ten years. I

have two years left. There's no way of knowing where I'll be then. Mrs. Sawyer only made plans to stay here for six to eight weeks. She wants to return back East. If she does that, I'll have to accompany her."

Night had fallen. Lavette grimaced, knowing she'd done most of the talking. This was the first time she'd told anyone the whole story. For the last eight years, she hadn't had a friend to confide in. She didn't want to think why she felt so comfortable with Josiah when she'd only known him such a short time. In her heart, she felt she'd known him forever. After all, he was the image of the handsome stranger who swept her off her feet in her childhood dreams.

A pack of coyotes began to sing their nightly chorus. The unearthly yips escalated, the voices of the younger coyotes making a sharp contrast with the more mature adults. Lavette knew many people hated the sound, but she found the cries a sign of freedom. Even the wild animals had more independence than she did. They could lift their muzzles and howl as much as they wanted, and no one could do a thing.

Josiah sighed. "I thought being an indentured servant wasn't done anymore — hadn't been done since the last century. I can't believe this."

Pulling her hand free, Lavette touched his cheek, making him look at her. His dark eyes swam with unshed tears.

"I felt a little bitter at first." She knew she had to make him understand. "Then I would remember that I helped my family by doing this. Who knows what would have happened to us if we had to continue on where we were? The last time I saw them, my mama was back to running the house. Papa loves working with horses again." She smiled. "I think you and Papa would get along well. You both have that interest in common."

He leaned his cheek against her hand, but she pulled back. "My only regret is that I can't have a relationship with anyone. I can be your friend for a short time, but that's all." Her heart begged him to understand what she was saying.

"But your family." Josiah's brow creased in a frown. "Don't you miss them?"

"Of course. Don't you miss your family?"

He nodded. "I guess I see your point. That isn't a good argument. I find that I want to get angry and say this isn't right."

"There's no need to fret." Lavette stood and stretched, arching her back to ease the ache. "I've come to terms with freedom, or the lack of it. Even when my time with this contract is up, I have the feeling I still won't be delivered. Something will happen. I don't know what, but I can feel it."

She picked up Josiah's discarded plate and cup. "We all have burdens to bear, and mine is being a bondwoman to some master or mistress. I can live with that. I have to."

Backing toward the door, she hoped he would leave. Her stomach ached from holding back her emotions. She wanted to lie on her bed in the dark where no one could hear her and cry. Talking to Josiah brought up the resentment she'd buried. She hadn't told him the truth. She would never get over the idea of being a slave and the indignation accompanying that. Inside, she would always long for freedom — even if she never found it.

"Wait, Lavette." Josiah reached her in two quick steps. "Let me pray with you about this. God didn't bring you all the way out here for no reason. He has a purpose, and I believe His purpose involves the two of us."

Anger bubbled up, making Lavette's

words come out in a bitter torrent. "I don't ask God about anything. He quit caring about me and my family a long time ago. For years my mama said Jesus would set us free and things would be better. Well, look what happened. My mama got sick, and I ended up in bondage again."

Pushing the door open, she flung her parting words in a hushed voice. "I can't stop you from praying, but don't ever ask me to pray with you." Stepping inside, only the thought of Mrs. Sawyer sleeping kept Lavette from slamming the door in his face.

Chapter 9

Josiah slipped the rod into the hot coals, twisting it with the tongs until the metal lay settled among the glowing embers. Next to the bar, he placed a crucible with iron to melt. His left hand automatically found the cord to the bellows. He pulled, sending a steady stream of air to intensify the heat. The coals glowed from reddish-orange to white hot. Tiny flames, lissome dancers, rose up and swayed across the embers in a graceful, ethereal rhythm. Mesmerized, Josiah heard nothing around him.

As he waited for the ore to heat so he could begin work on the nails and the new axe head one of his customers had ordered, Josiah tried to ignore the inner heaviness that weighed on him this morning. Lavette's parting words yesterday evening had kept him awake most of the night. He knew he could never marry someone who didn't share his love for and belief in Jesus Christ. All this time, he'd taken Lavette's faith for granted. He'd assumed she loved Jesus as much as he did. He should have known better. The voice of his mother reminding him that a young lady's spiritual beauty would always be more important than her physical charm rang through his mind.

When Lavette appeared at his smithy that first morning, he'd known she was a gift from God. He hadn't questioned, only accepted. Now he knew that he should have discussed her faith at the first opportunity rather than have his heart broken when he discovered her disbelief. How could he have been so blind? What should he do now?

Lifting the crucible from the fire, Josiah checked to see if the iron was ready, then placed the partially molten ore back in the heat. Using the tongs, he turned the iron bar. He couldn't seem to focus today. Of course, he hadn't been thinking right since Lavette walked into his life. She'd managed, in a very short time, to turn his reasoning upside down.

After running his hand over the smooth face of his anvil, Josiah went on to check over his tools. He knew the importance of caring for the implements of his trade.

He'd made most of them himself, although a few were ones his father had given him when he left home. With these tools and the knowledge he carried, he would always be able to make his way. His father had seen to that.

The long tongs fastened onto the glowing shaft. Josiah lifted the hot iron from the embers, careful to keep away from the sparks. The small scars dotting his bare arms bore testimony to the dangers of the flying ash and coal.

"That's what I like to see — a man hard at work."

Josiah swung around to grin at Conlon. "Have you thought of trying it for yourself, or do you spend so much time watching those soldiers of yours, you don't have time to do any physical labor?"

"A cruel blow." Conlon tried to act affronted, but the sparkle in his eyes told the truth. "You have no idea the mental anguish I suffer from forcing all those cavalrymen to do their jobs every day."

Josiah shook his head. Sometimes Conlon didn't have a serious bone in his body. That's one of the reasons they were able to stay so close. They seemed to both have the ability to laugh and forgive. Then too being brothers in faith helped build a strong bond between them. God had worked a miracle by giving him such wonderful friends.

"So, how many horses do I need to shoe for you today?" Josiah gave a light tug on the bellows rope, then moved away from the heat.

A wounded look crossed Conlon's face. "I didn't bring you work. It so happens I need a valuable opinion, and you were the first one I thought to ask."

"What have you done now? Is Glorianna making you sleep in the barn with the horse?"

Conlon chuckled. "With those twins walking and getting into everything, that might not be so bad." He pursed his mouth in a thoughtful expression. "Come to think of it, the horse doesn't pull my hair, climb all over me, or scream in my ear, and I never need to change his diapers."

"Your horse wears diapers?" Josiah raised his eyebrows, feigning surprise. "That must be an interesting sight."

Conlon's grin turned to a chuckle, then a roar of laughter. His eyes crinkled, tears of mirth winking in the light of the fire. Gasping, Conlon wiped his eyes with the back of his hand. "I have to admit that

116

would be a funny sight." He continued to chuckle. "No, my horse doesn't wear diapers. If he did, I would probably take him inside at night. I think he would be great at helping corral those kids of mine."

Glancing at the forge, Josiah could see he needed to check the heating metal. Tongs in hand, he picked up the bar and moved it to the edge of the fire. After placing the crucible next to the iron, he turned back to his friend.

"So, what kind of advice can I give you?"

"I'm interested in purchasing some new horses for the cavalry. I went to look at some yesterday, and I wanted to see if you know of them. Eduardo Villegas has them for sale. I know he's honest, because he's been selling cattle to the cavalry for a number of years. Now, he's raising horses too. Have you seen them?"

Josiah nodded. "I know Villegas. He has some fine stock. He's been working to build a herd for awhile now. I'd think he would be a good one to buy from. He treats his animals right. Do you want me to go with you to look them over?"

"I think I already had my mind made up, but if you get the chance to look at them, you might give me your opinion." Conlon rubbed the back of his neck. "His horses are a mite more money than some others, but they seem sound. I wanted to see what you thought before I spent the extra for them."

"He's been after me to do some work for him. When I'm there, I'll look over his stock."

Conlon gave Josiah a devilish grin. "Now that we have business out of the way, how's the sweetheart? Shall I have Glory and Kathleen start working on a wedding dress?"

Josiah resisted the urge to make a face. Instead, he turned to check the forge. With the tongs, he carefully plucked the crucible from the midst of the burning embers. After setting the fiery hot container on the bench, he lifted the lid and put it to one side. Heat waves undulated up from the molten mass. In a ritual he'd practiced since he was a boy, Josiah lifted the pot and poured the melted iron into the molds he had ready. Conlon stood silent, watching the whole process, a serious expression replacing the levity of moments before.

Placing the empty jar in its proper place, Josiah turned to inspect his work. He didn't want to ignore his friend, but right now, he wasn't sure he could talk about his relationship with Lavette. After last night there couldn't be any relationship, and that thought was eating a hole in his heart.

"Okay, Josiah." Conlon's hand on Josiah's arm halted him in midstep. "I think we need to sit down and talk. Have any coffee around here?" Conlon glanced to the corner of the smithy where Josiah usually had hot brew ready to share with a customer.

"I'll get you some." Josiah pulled free with little effort and filled two cups. This was the problem with having a good friend. Conlon could read him like a book. In a way, he wanted to confide in Conlon, knowing he would get godly advice. At least Conlon would care enough to listen; however, what he felt for Lavette seemed so precious, Josiah didn't know if he could bare his heart even to his best friend.

Conlon took a long sip of coffee and made a face. "When did you make this stuff — last week?"

Leaning back against the side of the shop, Josiah shrugged. "I can't afford to make fresh coffee every five minutes in case you show up and want some." He took a sip. "You could be right. This tastes like it's left over from a month ago." He chuckled, a hollow sound that echoed in his broken heart.

"So, care to talk?" Conlon blew the steam across the top of his cup, then slurped noisily. He grinned and winked at Josiah. "I can't do that at home. Glory would look daggers at me. Now, what happened between you and Miss Johnson? The last I heard, she was the best thing since store-bought boots. Isn't she as sweet as you first thought?"

Josiah couldn't help the smile that creased his cheeks. "Oh, she's sweet all right. I've never met a more delightful gal."

"Then what's the problem? She doesn't go for a big oaf like you?" Conlon grinned.

"I'd say she's a mite taken with me." Josiah rested his elbows on his knees, the steam from his coffee wafting past his eyes. "The problem is, last night when we were talking, I found out she and I don't share a faith in Jesus. In fact, she's carrying a mighty big grudge against God."

For several minutes, Conlon sat silent, sipping and listening as Josiah related the events of the previous evening. "She was so angry when I mentioned praying that she almost slammed the door in my face. I'll still pray for her, but I can't consider pursuing anything serious. Even if, as a child, she did believe in Jesus, right now she's full of resentment and anger toward Him."

"So, you're going to give up on her?" Conlon set his empty mug on the bench.

"I'm not giving up. I've been begging Jesus to help her all night and all day." Josiah tried not to be angry at his friend. "I don't know what more I can do."

"I apologize." Conlon gripped Josiah's shoulder. "I seem to remember a friend of mine telling me to be patient and let God have a chance to work. Why don't we agree to pray together for Miss Johnson? You know the power of that. I'll even get Glory and the Kirbys to join with us."

"I'd appreciate that." Josiah stood and stretched. He had to get back to work. "I don't know that there's any chance she's the right woman for me, but that doesn't matter as much as her getting over her anger at God."

Conlon stood and handed Josiah his cup. "You know, Glory and Kathleen have already visited her once. Maybe they could stop by again and invite her to our Sunday morning meeting. If the invitation comes from them, maybe she won't find it as easy to say no."

The heaviness in Josiah's heart eased. "I'll pray specifically that she'll agree to come." He nodded at Conlon. "Thanks. Tell Glory hello for me." Josiah turned and walked back into the smithy with a lighter step than he'd had since last evening.

Lavette folded the bread dough over and pushed, sending a whoosh of yeasty smell into the air. She folded and pushed again, kneading the pockets of air out of the dough, making it smooth. Patting the mound into a ball shape, she placed it on a bed of flour and covered the mass with a soft cloth to keep the flies away while the leavening worked.

On the counter near the stove, a batch of cinnamon rolls was rising, nearly ready to pop into the oven. Two pies cooled on the open windowsill. Ever since last night when she'd exploded at Josiah, Lavette couldn't seem to stay still. She'd gotten up early from a restless night and begun baking. The familiarity of the routine helped to calm her ragged nerves.

Guilt ate at her. She could recall her mother and father talking in hushed whispers about the Lord Jesus and how He would come to take them to gloryland one day. Her mother taught her songs about climbing a ladder into heaven and other spirituals. Their master didn't allow the slaves to have formal services, but even he couldn't stop the secret meetings that occurred after dark when they were supposed to be too tired to talk. Lavette could still remember curling up in a corner of the room, wide-eyed, as her parents and other couples would share bits of Scripture they'd learned. Early on she caught the excitement of a Savior who would one day deliver them. For years, along with many of her relatives and friends, she'd clung to that hope. Had she been wrong to turn her back on God when He let her down? Where were all those promises? Why had God said one thing, then done another? If she couldn't trust God to keep His word, then how could she trust Him with her life?

By the end of the War Between the States, she'd been sure Jesus was setting His people free. Then she would have all the privileges of independence like Miss Susannah. That hadn't happened. Instead, she and her family suffered even more, and within a short time she was once again a slave. Oh, they didn't call her that, but she was one all the same.

Anger churned in her stomach. She pushed away the bitterness and tried to recall her mother's face and the reason she'd given up so much for her family. They were worth the cost, weren't they? If she had the chance to choose again, she would do the same thing. Only this time she wouldn't go into servanthood with any misconception that Jesus would come along and rescue her. Reality had long ago overturned that delusion.

The tinkle of a bell chimed from the other room. Mrs. Sawyer must be finished with her lunch. Lavette took the cloth off the cinnamon buns and slid the pan into the oven. She wiped her hands on her apron and hurried down the hall.

"Thank you, Dear." Mrs. Sawyer gave a smile. "I can't tell you how wonderful I feel today. It must be this warm, dry air. I'd like to sit in the parlor for awhile and look out the window. Would you mind helping me?"

Lavette returned her mistress's smile. In the past days Mrs. Sawyer had made a vast improvement. A pink flush tinted her cheeks, and her eyes sparkled with life. Her cough had disappeared. Lavette couldn't remember the last time Mrs. Sawyer was this well.

"I think you've been enjoying your daughter and those sweet grandchildren." Lavette steadied Mrs. Sawyer with one arm holding her around the waist and the other on her closest shoulder. "This visit has done you a lot of good."

"I believe you're right." Mrs. Sawyer took several steps and stopped to rest, leaning against Lavette for support. "I think I shall get up every day and try walking a little farther. Maybe if I start sitting up more, I'll gain some strength."

"As long as you don't tire yourself too much." Lavette helped her through the door to the parlor and into the chair by the window. "Would you like me to bring a blanket for your lap? I don't want you chilling."

"That would be very nice." The light appeared to shine through Mrs. Sawyer's paper thin, blue-veined hands as she held them in the sunlight that streamed inside. Plucking a lap quilt from the back of a chair, Lavette spread the comforter over Mrs. Sawyer's legs, tucking the edge under to hold in the warmth.

An odd rapping issued from the front door. Mrs. Sawyer's countenance brightened. "Oh, I do hope that's Gretta come to visit. Did she plan to come today?"

"I don't believe she did." Lavette frowned. "I'll see who it is and be right back."

At the front door she stopped, her hand trembling on the latch. What if Josiah had come back? The thought made her heart leap even though she'd done her best to scare him away for good. The rapping began again. Lavette took a deep breath and pulled the door open. Her hand tightened on the wood. She couldn't speak. She began to quake — not from anticipation, but from fear.

Chapter 10

"Good day, Miss Johnson." Bertrand Mead's smooth tone sent dread racing through Lavette. He still held his silver-headed cane aloft, ready to rap on the door once more, should it close on him. "I came to speak with your mistress, if you'll let her know I'm here. She is available for company, isn't she?" His small eyes narrowed. "I've heard she's getting stronger and is able to receive callers."

Lavette opened her mouth, but nothing came out. The door latch cut into her palm, the pain easing some of the fear. She wanted to slam the door shut and pile every stick of furniture in the house against it to keep this man away. The devil himself couldn't have been much scarier.

"Well, may I come in?" He bent toward her, and she could smell again the cloying aroma of whatever he used after he washed. Her stomach roiled like she was rocking on a storm-tossed ship.

"Lavette, Dear, who's here?" At the sound of Mrs. Sawyer's quavery voice, Mead raised one eyebrow, the corner of his mouth lifting in a contemptuous smile.

"I'll go announce you." Lavette took a quick step back and started to shut the door. Mead inserted his cane, striking the door with an audible thump.

"I'll step inside while you notify Mrs. Sawyer of my presence." His shoes clicked smartly as he moved past her and slid the door closed behind him.

Lavette backed away, doing her best to repress a shudder as his slimy gaze flicked over her. Rounding the door to the parlor, she breathed a sigh of relief. Her whole body shook.

"Why, whatever is the matter, Girl? You look a little peaked." Mrs. Sawyer bent forward, peering intently at Lavette.

"I believe I've startled your servant without intending to, Ma'am."

Lavette whirled to find Mead standing in the doorway behind her. "Mrs. Sawyer, Mr. Bertrand Mead is here to see you." Her voice sounded hollow and shaky.

"What a pleasure. I don't get much company. Come in and sit down, young man."

Lavette moved to the side, hoping Mead

wouldn't touch her as he walked past. He crossed the room and bent over Mrs. Sawyer, lifting her hand for a gentleman's kiss.

"Good afternoon. I'm acquainted with your son-in-law, Paul Ashton. He talks so much about you, I decided to come by and see for myself if you are as wonderful as he says."

Mrs. Sawyer giggled. Lavette's stomach clenched, the contents threatening to come up.

"I'll have none of that flattery, Mr. Mead. Sit down here beside me. Lavette, why don't you bring us something? I'm sure Mr. Mead would enjoy some refreshments."

"Why yes, I would." Mead's eyes bored into Lavette, reminding her he intended to own her. "If I'm not mistaken, I smell something delicious baking. Paul's commented on your servant's excellent cooking skills. I'm sure they're only the beginning of her talents."

Lavette's hands shook so much, she almost dropped the pan of rolls as she pulled them from the oven. The sweet cinnamon scent that she loved nauseated her this time. What was Mead doing here? What did he really want? The possible answers frightened her so much, she wanted to run.

She took her time putting the cups, coffee, and buns on a tray. The thought of facing Mead again was more than she could bear. Perhaps she could accidentally spill coffee on him and he would have to leave. Lavette shook her head and sighed. The way her hands were shaking, the spilling wouldn't be hard to imagine.

Picking up the tray, she steeled herself for the ordeal of seeing Mead again. The question of his real reason for calling on Mrs. Sawyer nagged at her as she carried the refreshments into the parlor.

"Ah, here's Lavette with some of her famous cinnamon buns. This girl is a wonder." Mrs. Sawyer gave her a lopsided smile, but Lavette could see the tired lines beginning to show around her mouth and eyes. As soon as the pair finished eating, she would suggest that her mistress needed to rest and get Mead out of the house.

Mrs. Sawyer waved away the roll and coffee Lavette offered to serve her. She knew the lady had trouble eating when she began to tire. Although she grew stronger every day, Mrs. Sawyer still didn't have the stamina for long visits. Lavette forced her face to be void of expression as Mead deliberately caressed her hand as he took the plate from her. She straightened and moved toward the door.

"I'll be back in a few minutes." Lavette faced her mistress. "You'll need to rest soon."

"Let me visit a little longer." Mrs. Sawyer seemed to wilt more each moment. "This gentleman is telling me about his business prospects. We can talk a few more minutes, then perhaps you can return another day, Mr. Mead."

Bertrand Mead caught Lavette's gaze. She hurried from the room. Resting her forehead against the painted wall of the hallway, Lavette let out a slow breath. She hadn't feared a man this much since she'd gotten away from the plantation. Mead reminded her of Miss Susannah's father — the way he used to watch her and try to catch her alone. His touch had been as repulsive as Mead's.

She tried to ignore the low rumble of voices as she fought to get her emotions under control. Whatever Mead had to say about himself, she didn't want to listen to his lies. Lavette knew he continued to flatter her employer from the number of girlish giggles issuing from a woman who should be old enough to see Mead's compliments for what they were — lies.

"I really must be on my way." Mead's words cut through Lavette's thoughts. "Before I go, I would like to speak with you about your young servant, Miss Johnson. I had the pleasure of hearing her sing. She has the voice of an angel."

Lavette wanted to run. She knew she shouldn't be listening, but her feet seemed rooted to the spot.

"Because my other business ventures are doing so well, I thought I should try to bring some of the sophistication of the eastern cities to our little town."

"What are you thinking of doing?"

"I would like to start a theater of sorts to present the arts to the citizens of Tucson. I thought perhaps Miss Johnson could sing for us as a regular part of the entertainment."

Lavette could hear the frown in Mrs. Sawyer's voice. "I'm not sure I approve of that, but there won't be a chance, anyway. We leave to return home in a few weeks. Lavette won't be here to perform."

"Paul did mention that you would be returning to your home. At first, I thought to offer Miss Johnson the opportunity to remain here when you leave, but Paul says she has a contract to fulfill. I came today to ask you to consider allowing me to purchase her agreement before you leave."

"Why, I don't know that I can do that." Mrs. Sawyer sounded shocked.

"I'm not asking you to give me an answer today, dear lady. I'm only requesting that you consider my offer. You might speak with your daughter and son-in-law too. Now, you look tired. I'll see myself out, and you get some rest. I'll be back to visit soon."

Before Lavette could move, Mead rounded the corner into the hall. His narrow gaze fastened on her. The sneer lifting the corner of his mouth gave him a triumphant appearance. She flattened against the wall as he started past. He stopped. She stared in silent terror as he roughly stroked his thumb over her cheek. "You'll be mine." He mouthed the words, gave her a feral smile, stalked to the door, and disappeared.

An hour later, Lavette eased the back door closed behind her. She still couldn't believe the control she'd shown as she prepared Mrs. Sawyer for her nap and finished putting the bread in the pans to rise. Any thoughts of Mead and his threats and conversation with her mistress were blocked for the moment. She'd floated through the hour in an air of unreality, feeling like she watched herself at work, rather than doing the chores in person. Now, the truth began to seep inside. Her stomach knotted, fear replacing the calm.

She wondered if she could run away. Maybe the little bit of money she'd saved over the years would be enough to purchase a ticket for the stage. Hope sank as she realized her funds weren't enough to get home to her family, and anywhere else she went would leave her vulnerable to other types like Mead. Who would hire an unknown girl with no visible means and no references?

Hurrying across the backyard, Lavette began to wander the quiet side streets. Walking always helped her think, and right now she had to come up with a plan to escape before Mead figured a way to make her his. Despair clutched at her with painful fingers. *Oh, Papa, I need you. I don't know what to do. You wouldn't let him hurt me. Was I wrong to become a bondservant when you didn't want me to? Is this the cost of disobedience?*

Tears blinded her. She hurried on, her head lowered, not watching where she was going. Dashing a hand across her watering eyes, Lavette did her best to stop the panic welling up inside.

"Well, well, what have we here?" Mead's question stopped her cold. He stood beside a tree, his hands resting on top of his cane. His eyes raked over her in a way that made her want to hide. She felt like a rabbit caught in a snare, with no strength to run.

In two strides, Mead stood beside her, close enough that she could smell alcohol on his breath. She tried to turn away to avoid the unpleasant smell. Mead's well-manicured fingers grasped her arm, forcing her to face him. Her heart pounded.

"Looking for me, were you?" He chuckled, a predatory rumble that held no mirth. "You must be eager to begin working for me. I know your singing will please the crowds, but I'll train you in other areas too."

Lavette gasped. Jerking back, she tried to break free. His hold didn't loosen. Why did this street have to be so deserted right now? Why hadn't she gone where there would be other people? Did it matter? They would probably refuse to help her anyway.

"Oh, no, my sweet. I'm thinking I should give you an early trial. Why don't you accompany me? My Jackrabbit Saloon isn't too far. You can give the boys a song or two." He slipped his cane under his arm and began to run his fingers down her forearm to her wrist. "Maybe you can even give me a little private entertainment." He began to pull her close.

Pure panic swept over her. Lavette jerked back. She kicked, and her foot met his shin. Mead grimaced. His grip tightened. She bent forward, trying to ease the ache in her arm.

"Let me go." She couldn't look at him. She already knew what she would see in his eyes. "I need to get back before Mrs. Sawyer wakes up. She'll expect me to be there."

"Oh, we won't keep you all that long, my dear. I simply want to give the men who visit my establishment a taste of what's to come." He took a firm hold of her upper arm, propelling her down the street. "This way when I convince your mistress to sell me your contract, the men will be waiting and eager. Word will spread about your wonderful voice and beauty."

She wanted to shout at him. She wanted to yell, *I can't sing for you. I won't.* Years of slavery and beatings when she refused to follow her master's orders left her unable to find the courage to say the words. Instead, the clench of foreboding made her too afraid to keep pace. Despite his tight hold on her arm, her steps flagged enough that he too began to slow. A few men passed by, but rather than help her, they averted their faces.

"If you think going at the pace of an ant will give you time, you're wrong." Alcohol fumes made her wrinkle her nose as he tugged her close. "I'm going to get hold of you and never let you go."

Lavette stumbled as Mead released her. His arm swept around her back, yanking her against him again. Like an iron band, he held her tight. She couldn't breathe. He began to lower his mouth. Lavette tried to kick and squirm to no avail. She turned her head. His lips brushed her cheek. Mead cursed.

"Let her go, Mead."

At the soft-spoken command, Mead looked up. His grip eased, but Lavette still couldn't get away.

"Why, Deputy, we're only having a little discussion. There's no need to interrupt."

"Let the lady go."

Mead's eyes flashed. His lips thinned. Lavette felt his hold loosen a bit more, and she began to push away. Mead released her. She stumbled back and would have fallen if not for the hands that caught her. She could see the star pinned to the man's chest.

"Now get on back to the hole you crawled out of, Mead." Anger gave the deputy's voice a menacing quality. "One of these days, you'll make a mistake, and I'll be waiting. I want you to leave this young lady alone. Understand?"

"Why, I had no intention of hurting Miss Johnson." Mead smirked. "I was acting the gentleman and showing her around. Good day." He tipped his hat and strolled away, the silver of his walking cane sparkling in the sunlight.

"Miss Johnson, is it?"

Lavette nodded. The deputy had a kind voice when he wasn't talking to Mead. She still didn't dare look up.

"I believe my wife met you the other day. I'm Deputy Quinn Kirby. My wife is Kathleen. She said she and Glorianna Sullivan dropped by to see you."

"Yes, Suh, they did."

"Are you all right? Mead didn't hurt you, did he?"

Rubbing her arm, Lavette knew she would have bruises. Those would heal. The hurt Mead intended to inflict wouldn't mend easily.

"I'm fine." That wasn't true, but Lavette didn't want to say more to the deputy. The realization that she was safe sank in. Her knees began to quake. She wasn't sure she could even walk. A lump lodged in her throat. Tears burned in her eyes. She knew she had to get out of here before she began to cry. The strain from the afternoon's events proved too much. A lone tear trickled down her cheek and dripped onto her dress. She turned her head away, hoping the deputy hadn't noticed.

Deputy Kirby picked up her hand and tucked it into the crook of his arm. "Why don't you come with me?" He acted as if he didn't know she was crying, yet he must have noticed. "I left home a few minutes ago. Kathleen and Glorianna were having a visit. If I'm not mistaken, you could use a lady to talk to about now."

She'd gone off without her hanky. Lavette sniffed, wishing the tears would stop. They came harder. She bit her lip. Deputy Kirby opened a door and ushered her into a kitchen that smelled of fresh-baked bread and roasting meat. She wanted to turn and run the other way.

"Why, look who's come for a visit, Kathleen."

From the corner of her eye, Lavette

could see Glorianna's red hair as the small woman swept toward her.

"Welcome to my house, Lavette. I'm glad you could come over." Kathleen stopped by Lavette, stretched up, and kissed her husband on the cheek. Lavette heard the door close behind her. A dam broke. Sobs began to wrack her body. She barely felt the arms that hugged her close, giving her the comfort she desperately needed.

Chapter 11

"Lavette, what's wrong?" Kathleen's voice was soothing. Her hand rubbed circles on Lavette's back, seeming to understand the ache she had there. "Come on in and sit down."

Sobs still shook her body as the two women led the way to the kitchen table. Lavette could see that Kathleen had been the one holding onto her. Glorianna thrust a hanky into Lavette's curled fist. Mopping the tears and wiping her dripping nose, Lavette wished she could crawl under the table. She didn't even know these women well. How could she have behaved this way? Her mother would never understand.

"Would you like a glass of water or a cup of coffee?" Kathleen sat close, her hand still stroking Lavette's shoulder.

Cool water sounded so good, Lavette almost groaned at the thought. How could she ask this woman to wait on her, though?

She was the servant. A white woman didn't bring something to a black person. She shook her head, then held her breath, trying to stop the hiccups that always seemed to follow crying. If she could only get hold of her emotions, she would be able to thank Kathleen and Glorianna and leave.

"Did we mention the other day that we're friends of Josiah's?" Glorianna pulled a chair close on the other side of Lavette. "He told us you haven't seen your family in a number of years. I would imagine that's pretty hard, not being able to talk with any family. Then you come out here to Tucson, where you don't know a soul."

"Lavette, we'd like to be your friends." Kathleen's voice had a soothing quality that reminded Lavette of her mother. "I don't know what happened, but something upset you a lot. Is Mrs. Sawyer all right?"

Lavette nodded.

"Are you having trouble working for her?"

Lavette shook her head. The hiccups and sobs stopped, but she still trembled, remembering the way Mead had looked at her and touched her.

Glorianna brushed a lock of Lavette's hair back from her face. "Did you fall or do something to hurt yourself?"

Once more, Lavette shook her head. These women seemed so kind, but she couldn't bring herself to talk to them. She hadn't wanted her mama this badly since she was a young child, and she wasn't sure her mother would know what to do about Mead.

Kathleen patted her shoulder once more and rose. "I'd like a cup of coffee. Would you like one, Glory?"

Still smoothing Lavette's hair in a gesture so calming, Lavette thought she might start purring if she were a cat, Glorianna said, "That sounds good. I might like a little water too."

Dishes clinked as Kathleen busied herself near the stove and the water bucket. Before long, she set two cups of water on the table in front of Lavette and Glorianna, returning moments later with coffee for each of them. From the aroma, Lavette knew the coffee must be freshly brewed. Kathleen made one more trip, bringing back the same drinks for herself. Lavette knew they were doing this to make her feel comfortable. She marveled that they would consider waiting on her like this.

"Thank you." The whispered words came from her. She picked up the water and took a long sip. The cool liquid soothed the ache in her throat. She swallowed some more before placing the glass back on the table.

"Lavette, can you look at me?" Kathleen took Lavette's hand in hers as she spoke. Lavette glanced up. The gold and green of Kathleen's eyes mesmerized her. She'd never seen anyone with that color of eyes before. Of course, she rarely looked at a white person. She knew better.

"My husband told me when Josiah first met you, Bertrand Mead happened by." Kathleen's hands squeezed as a chill raced through Lavette. "Has he been bothering you again?" Kathleen's soft question pricked Lavette. Could these women understand?

"I need to get back home before Mrs. Sawyer wakes up from her nap. She'll be expecting me." Lavette began to quake at the thought of walking home alone. Even though it wasn't far, Mead could be anywhere. She forced herself to stand. "Thank you so much." Her voice shook.

Glorianna stood and stretched. "I hate to say this, Kathleen, but I'd best get home too. The twins are probably awake, and Alicia will need help with them." She touched Lavette on the arm. "My house isn't far from yours. Shall we walk together?"

Gratitude made Lavette's knees weak. "That'd be fine." She couldn't keep the relief out of her tone.

As they made their way down the dusty streets, Glorianna kept up a light chatter. She talked about her husband and the new fort. They would be moving there soon. He'd wanted to live there already, but Glorianna had begged him to wait until after Kathleen had her baby. They were cousins, and Glorianna wanted to stay close for now.

She talked about her twins, Andrew and Angelina, and the trials and blessings of having babies. Lavette learned more about Glorianna and Conlon than she would have thought possible in such a short time. Although she hadn't said a word, Lavette felt warmed by Glorianna's offer of friendship. This wasn't the type of companion Miss Susannah wanted. Glorianna seemed to care about knowing Lavette, something Lavette had never had from a white woman.

They reached the door of Mrs. Sawyer's house. Without looking at Glorianna, Lavette spoke. "Thank you. I baked some pies and rolls today. Would you like some to take home to your family? We have more than we can eat with just the two of us."

"Why, I do believe I'd love that. I doubt if Alicia's gotten much done today in the way of baking. She's had her hands full while I was at Kathleen's."

Not wanting to disturb Mrs. Sawyer if she still slept, Glorianna insisted on staying outside. Lavette brought out a pie and rolls wrapped in a cloth to keep the flies and dust from getting on them. "Thank you for walking me home."

Balancing the sweets on one hand, Glorianna gave Lavette's fingers a gentle squeeze. "We'll talk again soon. Before I go, I do want to invite you over to my house this Sunday morning."

"Me?"

"Yes, you. We don't have a church here in Tucson that we can attend. Some of us get together on Sunday. We sing, share Bible verses, and pray. Then we all eat together." Lavette could hear the smile in Glorianna's voice.

"I don't usually attend church."

"Well, this is more like friends getting together. Please come."

Lavette nodded. "I'll try, but only if Mrs. Sawyer's daughter will be coming to take her to her house."

"I hope you'll be there." Glorianna gave Lavette's fingers another squeeze, then walked off down the path. Lavette watched her go, Glorianna's red-gold hair shimmering in the light. Could she trust this woman to be her friend? Her heart wanted to say yes, but her experience said no. The hope that started to blossom faded at that thought. She had no friend, no one to confide in, and right now, she needed someone.

Josiah whistled as he strode down the street toward Conlon's house. Sunday, his day of rest, always made him want to make music. Then too Josiah knew he needed the day off.

This had been a rough week. As much as he liked Lavette, he hadn't been by to see her after their talk about praying. He'd struggled with that decision, especially after his conversation with Conlon. Still, he felt God wouldn't want him becoming attached to a woman who was too angry at God to pray.

Quinn had stopped by on Thursday to tell him about rescuing Lavette from Mead. Josiah had to stop work and spend time alone in prayer to keep from looking Mead up and confronting him. Mead would never listen to him. He might end up doing more harm than good.

For the first time since becoming a Christian, Josiah felt as if he were walking alone. Always before, God seemed so close. In prayer time, he could feel the presence of the Holy Spirit. When he went through a trial, Jesus was right there, lighting the way and giving him comfort to carry on. This time, Josiah couldn't sense God anywhere. Maybe this morning's meeting with the other Christians would help.

Striding up the path, Josiah glanced up at the Sullivans' porch. A slight figure stood at the door, her hand raised to knock. She lowered her fist, raised it, then lowered it again. She turned and began to leave.

"Lavette?" Josiah couldn't believe what he was seeing. She started and nearly dropped the dish she held.

"Oh, you scared me." She looked embarrassed as she shuffled to one side, allowing him to go past her.

"Isn't anybody home?" Josiah frowned. "We were supposed to have our meeting here."

"I think they're home." Lavette stared at the ground, her fingers kneading the cloth covering what smelled like fried chicken.

Josiah's mind crept back to the times when he stood by his mother as the pieces of chicken popped and spattered in a pan full of grease. The memory brought a strong ache for home and family that he hadn't experienced in years.

Shaking off the reverie, Josiah recalled Conlon saying Glorianna intended to invite Lavette to the service. "Are you here for the Sunday get-together?" He smiled and guided her to the door, his hand on her back. "Come on. I'll help you in and introduce you around."

Lavette glanced up, her eyes wide and fearful. "I don't know."

"Come on." Josiah chuckled. "Remember, the only ones who bite here are Andrew and Angelina. Since they're babies, you can't blame them." He guided her up the steps. "Take warning, though. Don't stick your finger in the mouth of a child that young."

She giggled, a wonderful sound. "I don't recall my brother so much when he was a baby but those girls were terrible. They chewed everything. My papa said they were worse than a whole litter of puppies."

He laughed. He hadn't been this light-hearted since the last time he'd seen her. How he wanted this to mean she was changing toward God! Maybe she would hear something this morning that would help her get rid of her anger and bitterness — something that would help her make peace with Him.

The Sullivans' parlor couldn't hold many more people. A pleasant buzz of conversation wound through the air. A mixture of smells emanated from the kitchen area: meats, spices, and sweets. The aroma of cinnamon reminded Josiah of the first day he met Lavette. He took his hand from her back to keep from turning the touch into a caress.

"Lavette, I'm so glad you could come." Glorianna threaded her way through the gathering to greet them. She took Lavette's free hand and patted it.

"Does this mean you aren't glad to see me?" Josiah tried to look offended.

"Oh, Josiah, don't get your feathers ruffled." Glorianna wrinkled her nose. "We see you all of the time, and you know how special you are." She smiled at Lavette. "If I'm not mistaken, you've brought fried chicken to share. That smells delicious."

"Yes, Ma'am." Lavette's response could barely be heard over the noise of the crowd. "Where would you like me to put the dish?"

"I'll take it for you." Glorianna reached out.

Lavette glanced up, her eyes wide, the whites giving her a look of absolute terror. "Oh, no, Ma'am. I — you have —" Her gaze skimmed the room before settling on Josiah's face. The pleading look in her eyes begged him to intervene.

"I'll show her where to put the chicken." Josiah hoped Glorianna would understand Lavette's fear of having someone else waiting on her. He grinned to lighten the moment. "I might even have to sample a piece. Maybe two."

Hands on hips, Glorianna glared at him. "Don't you dare, Josiah Washington. If I know you, once you start, you won't stop until everything in there has been tasted." She gave Lavette a look of mock exasperation, although Josiah wasn't sure Lavette noticed since her gaze was once again directed toward the floor. "I'll let him show you, Lavette, but you keep a close eye on him. Don't let him eat all our lunch before we even have the services."

The kitchen table and every other available space was piled with cloth-covered dishes and baskets of food. Josiah couldn't stop his stomach from protesting the fact that he could only look and smell, but not

151

eat. With only coffee for breakfast, he knew he might be embarrassed during the quiet moments of the meeting. Perhaps he could slip just one piece of chicken. He peeked in Lavette's direction and saw that she watched him, a knowing smile lifting the corners of her mouth.

"You wouldn't really tell on me, would you?" He started to lift the corner of the cloth over the chicken.

"Oh, no, you don't." She swatted his hand. "I remember my papa trying the very same thing. Mama always laughed and slapped his hand."

"What did your papa do?"

She grinned and tugged his arm away from the dish. "Well, he didn't starve to death."

Josiah gave an exaggerated sigh. "Come on. We'd best get back before they start, or Glorianna will be thinking I am sampling all the goodies." He gestured at the door, but Lavette hesitated. She glanced at him, then at the floor. "Hey, what's wrong?"

"I don't feel like I belong here. Are you sure my coming is all right?"

He put a finger under her chin, tipping her head back until her gaze met his. "Lavette, we're all glad you're here. Believe me, Glorianna wouldn't have invited you if she didn't want you to come." He began to escort her out, then stopped.

"One more thing." He waited until she looked at him. "You don't have to always examine the floor." He smiled to take the sting from the words. "You can look at these people and not be afraid. Maybe if you see their expressions, you'll be more comfortable speaking with them. God has blessed these Christians with a love for all people." He could feel her withdraw at the thought and waited to give her time to adjust to the new idea.

"I don't think I can." Lavette peered at him, her cinnamon eyes bright. "I'm so afraid sometimes."

Josiah's heart ached as he pulled Lavette close. He didn't want to think about what she'd gone through to make her so fearful of others. Leaning his cheek against her head, he whispered, "Stay close to me. Everything will be fine."

Chapter 12

Squeezed in beside Josiah in one corner of the room, Lavette tried to make herself even smaller, hoping no one would notice her. What had possessed her this morning? Yes, she'd made a promise of sorts to Glorianna. When Mrs. Sawyer announced that she planned to spend the day at her daughter's house, Lavette felt obligated to attend the service here. She even got permission to fix food to bring. Now, she wished she'd stayed home alone. Josiah was the only one here whom she knew very well, and he'd seemed to be avoiding her lately.

Peeking at the faces of the people clustered in the room, Lavette couldn't help wondering about those gathered here, as each seemed to have a look of excited expectation. Then again, why shouldn't they? Other than Josiah, none of the people in this room would have ever suffered the indignity of being bound. To her, God appeared to be the deity for this kind of people. They had every convenience and comfort. He provided well for them while her people suffered all sorts of trials.

Josiah leaned forward and clasped his hands together. Lavette moved to the side, allowing his broad back to hide her further. She twisted her hanky with her fingers to keep from touching him. The thought of resting her cheek against his back, the comfort that would bring, seemed so real she could almost feel the rough cotton of his shirt against her face.

Conlon stood. The conversation died away. An expectant hush settled over the room broken only by the whine of a baby unsure at the sudden change. "Glory and I want to welcome you all to our house. I've asked Josiah to lead the singing this week because we all know he's the only one who can carry a tune." Conlon grinned and everyone chuckled. Gesturing at Josiah, Conlon sat back down.

"Before we begin, I'd like to introduce you to someone new. In case you haven't met her, this is Lavette Johnson." Josiah reached back and plucked Lavette from her hiding place, pulling her forward so everyone in the room could stare at her. She wanted to die, yet at the same time she was filled with wonder that these people were willing to let Josiah speak up like that.

"Miss Johnson is here for a few weeks, and we hope she will join us often."

A spattering of applause met his statement. Lavette tried to look at the people. She'd been introduced to a few of them before being seated, but she knew she would never be able to put names with faces since she hadn't looked up at them. No matter what Josiah said, she couldn't do that. Even after they'd been given freedom at the end of the war, her family always had to show reverence for white folks by lowering their gaze when in the presence of a person of authority. Relief raced through Lavette when Josiah took his hand from her arm, allowing her to sink back behind him once more. From this vantage point, she could peek out at the men and women nestled together like birds in a nest. One of the men across the room seated next to a woman who looked like she'd eaten a green crabapple, stared back at Lavette, a strange expression on his puff-cheeked face. Lavette ducked back behind Josiah, wondering if she'd seen the man before.

Josiah began to lead the singing. Most of the songs weren't familiar to Lavette, so she sat silently, listening to Josiah's strong bass. He had a wonderful voice. She began to relax, lulled by the sound of music. Her father used to say that the only way to quiet her when she was an infant was to sing. For as long as she could recall, music brought out her heart and soul. She could hear a song in everyday noises that most people ignored.

The hymns ended and Conlon stood. "Glory and I have been studying the story of Joseph in the book of Genesis. I know most of you are familiar with the tale of how Joseph was a favorite of his father, Jacob. His brothers were so jealous, they sold him into slavery and told Jacob that Joseph died."

Conlon glanced down at Glorianna. She smiled and nodded. Lavette thought he must not be used to standing up and speaking before others like this. Longing stabbed through Lavette as she watched Glorianna's obvious devotion to her husband. As Conlon spoke, Glorianna's eyes shone with love. *Some day I want to feel that way about a man.* Brushing the thought away, Lavette turned her attention back to Conlon's dissertation.

"As a young boy, Joseph had several dreams about his brothers and father bowing down to him. Knowing those dreams came from God, I wondered if he got discouraged during his years in bondage. He even spent time in prison for something he didn't do."

Watching Josiah, with his open Bible on his lap, nodding at Conlon's account of Scripture, Lavette could see he wasn't upset or angry at all. Why did she feel such anger toward God? Hadn't Joseph suffered in slavery? She could picture Joseph being enraged at his brothers and at the unjust sentence he received. If those dreams truly came from God, then Joseph deserved to be mad. She had chosen to remain in servitude for a good reason, but Joseph had no choice. Lavette couldn't recall the story in detail, but she knew if she were Joseph, she would never forgive her brothers.

"I know a lot of people who have been betrayed by relatives or friends. They usually struggle with resentment, hatred, and anger. Joseph didn't have those feelings, and I intend to show you how I know that." Conlon ran a hand through his hair, leaving some of it to stick up in spikes. Glorianna started to rise, as if she would smooth his hair down. Kathleen, seated next to Glorianna, put a hand on her arm. Glorianna settled back in her chair, an amused twinkle in her eye.

"God began to bless Joseph. I think He did that because Joseph, rather than think of himself and allow those negative feelings toward those who betrayed him, tried to trust God with his life. After years in prison, Joseph became a very powerful man in Egypt because of God's plan.

"Finally, Joseph was able to confront his brothers. He had power over them. In fact, his dream came true: His brothers had to bow down to him." Conlon rubbed the back of his neck, staring at the page open in his Bible. "You know, I've thought and thought about this story. I can't imagine being as godly as Joseph. Is everyone familiar with what Joseph said to his brothers after their father's death?" Conlon paused. A few heads nodded, indicating they knew the verse he referred to. "I'd like to read this part to you."

As Conlon ran his finger down the page to find the verse, Lavette shifted forward on the seat. She couldn't wait to hear what Joseph had to say. He'd been a slave and unfairly imprisoned. They shared something in common. Surely, what he said would reflect her feelings, too.

Conlon cleared his throat. " 'And Joseph said unto them, Fear not: for am I in the place of God? But as for you, ye thought evil against me; but God meant it unto good, to bring to pass, as it is this day, to save much people alive. Now therefore fear ye not: I will nourish you, and your little ones. And he comforted them, and spake kindly unto them.' "

Stunned, Lavette ignored the murmured comments of the others in the room. Joseph let them off without any blame? Had she heard right? Did Joseph say it was all right for him to be made a slave and thrown into prison because God planned it that way? *If that's true, then what about me and my family, God? Did You intend our slavery to be for our good? I can't believe that.* Lavette fought the familiar anger coursing through her. For so long, she'd blamed God for all the terrible things that happened to her. Now she had a Scripture to show He was responsible. Even so, she couldn't understand why, and she couldn't seem to keep her anger. Instead, a hollow ache filled her.

Conlon raised a hand, and the whispered conversations faded away. "I've had to think this week about all the times I've blamed others for my circumstances, when all along maybe God had a bigger plan. I have the feeling if I'd stayed at home as a young man, I would never have met Jesus in a personal way. Even though I had a lot of rough years, I'm grateful for what I went through simply because God taught me so much. Glory feels the same way. I'd like to open a discussion this morning, where we can share how God used the trials in our lives to help bring us closer to Him."

Finished speaking, Conlon sat down. Glorianna gave him a loving touch on the shoulder, and he winked at her. She slipped her small hand into his, and Lavette could imagine how wonderful that would feel. Glimpsing at Josiah's work-roughened hands, she thought of the way her father's callused palms felt on her as a child. What she wouldn't give to feel a comforting touch right now. She was so confused.

Kathleen began to share her story, telling how her mother was ashamed to have a daughter born with a birthmark. She told of the years of hiding, too embarrassed to let people see her face, and how God taught her compassion for others because of what she endured.

Deputy Kirby told of the anger and hatred he carried with him and how God showed him the need to forgive others. Unbeknownst to him, the man Quinn despised married his sister. If he hadn't met Jesus before he went back home and discovered that truth, he might have been responsible for misery in his sister's life. He smiled and picked up his wife's hand, saying he was grateful to God for using the trials to bring him and Kathleen together.

Several others shared a testimony of God leading them through difficult times and the resulting good that came from it. Lavette wanted to scoff because none of the ones who were talking had ever been a slave, yet after the story of Joseph, she couldn't say anything. He had been a slave and not only forgave, but when his brothers felt guilty over what they'd done, Joseph comforted them and took care of them and their families.

The sound of Josiah's stomach rumbling brought Lavette out of her reverie. He grinned at her. She bit her lip to keep from laughing, wondering if anyone else heard.

"I think we should end the meeting with a song, then eat before Josiah starves." A spattering of chuckles followed Conlon's announcement.

"Josiah, why don't we try that song you taught us this week?" Glorianna and Kathleen spoke at the same time. They grinned at each other and Glorianna continued. "We can do all the verses if you have the strength."

"I can probably manage." Josiah rubbed his stomach. "I'll do much better if you promise I can be first in line for lunch."

"Oh, no, you don't." Quinn glowered at Josiah in mock anger. "We want some food left for us."

Josiah held up a hand in surrender. "I promise to save you a little. After all, I wouldn't want to be arrested for stealing all the grub." They all laughed.

"Like I told the Sullivans and the Kirbys, I hadn't heard this song for years. In fact, I forgot I even knew it until I heard Lavette singing one day. Hearing the words brought back memories from when my mama and her friends used to sing this." Josiah flashed Lavette a wide smile. His dark gaze warmed her.

"My Father, how long, my Father, how long, my Father, how long, poor sinner suffer here?"

The people began to join in with Josiah. Lavette listened a moment to the familiar song she'd learned as a young child. Closing her eyes, she could see her mother sitting in the rocking chair with a baby in her lap, singing "My Father" in a soft voice. Letting the melody take over her soul, Lavette joined her high, clear soprano to Josiah's bass.

"We'll soon be free, we'll soon be free, we'll soon be free, de Lord will call us home."

The second verse ended. Lavette drew a breath to begin the chorus when she realized she and Josiah were the only ones singing. Every eye in the room was trained on the two of them. Kathleen, Glorianna, and their husbands were staring open-mouthed. Chagrined, Lavette stopped and sank back to hide once more.

"Lavette." Glorianna came and knelt on the floor by Lavette's feet, waiting until Lavette looked up. "You have the most beautiful voice I've ever heard. You and Josiah are wonderful together. Please sing some more." Her green gaze held Lavette's.

"I'm not used to having everybody looking at me." Lavette's throat scratched with dryness.

"Well, you'd better get used to it." A chill filled the warm room as the tight-lipped woman across the room spoke up.

"Whatever do you mean by that, Mrs. Laughlin?" Glorianna looked over her shoulder at the older woman.

"I've heard where she's planning to sing." The woman's mouth looked even more pinched. Beside her, the man with the heavy jowls leered at Lavette, then, when the woman glanced at him, changed to an expression of indignation.

Mortified, Lavette couldn't imagine what the woman was talking about. Peering at the woman and the man next to her, Lavette thought again that she'd seen him somewhere before. Her mind flashed back to the day in the mercantile when Bertrand Mead confronted her. He'd dragged her back to where there were several men, telling them she would be performing for him. This man had been there — in the mercantile.

A cacophony of confusion reigned in the room as men and women began to question one another. The discussion grew in volume until Quinn stood. Although he wasn't a huge man, his presence commanded their attention. Quiet settled over the gathering.

"Mrs. Laughlin, Miss Johnson is a friend and guest. We'd like to know what you're implying with your comments."

The thin woman sat erect, her black clothes and thin face giving her the look of a bird of prey about to dive on some unsuspecting creature. "My Lyle came home the other day and told me what happened at the mercantile. This woman came in, supposedly to buy some things for her employer. She was really there to meet with Bertrand Mead, the owner of those heathen establishments." Her glare bored into Lavette like red-hot bullets. "Mead even introduced her to the men in the store. He bragged about how her sweet singing would bring him all sorts of money. I think it's a shame she had the gall to come to our meeting today."

Dead silence followed the woman's accusations. Lavette could feel the chair pressing into her back as she tried to sink from sight. These were all lies, yet no one in this room knew her well. Who would they be willing to believe — someone they'd only met recently or a long-time friend? She knew the answer to that question before she even asked.

Chapter 13

Josiah surged to his feet. Conlon shot him a warning glance. Glorianna appeared ready to spit fire at the Laughlins. Coming up out of his chair with an air of grace, Conlon moved to stand beside Quinn, effectively making a block between Mrs. Laughlin and Lavette. Josiah understood now. Conlon and Quinn would handle the affront; he should be there for Lavette. She would need someone to lean on right now.

He sank into his seat and half-turned so he could keep one eye on the proceedings, yet still see Lavette. She huddled against the chair back, her eyes downcast. Her lower lip trembled, her tiny white teeth making a sharp contrast as they hit into the lip in an obvious attempt to control her emotions.

Placing one of his hands over her clenched ones, Josiah could feel her tension. She must be on the verge of breaking down. Over the last several months, their group had tolerated the Laughlins' sporadic visits, hoping to reach them. Now, Josiah wished they'd been less congenial. As she'd done with others before, Mrs. Laughlin deliberately attacked Lavette with what he knew to be lies.

Josiah noted most of the room's occupants were involved in the discussion going on between Conlon, Quinn, and the Laughlins. He brought his head close to Lavette's, hoping she would realize their conversation would be private even in such a crowded place.

"You okay?" He could feel her trembling and wanted to wrap her in his arms. "This is not the first time Mrs. Laughlin has attacked someone. No one will listen to her."

"They're lies." A tear rolled down Lavette's cheek. Josiah wiped the drop with his thumb.

"I know she's lying. So do several of the others here. Gossip travels fast in this town. We've heard two stories: the one Mead told and the truth. The Christians will listen to the truth."

"They'll never believe my story against that of a white woman." Lavette's hurt made him ache.

His thumb caressed her cheek as he

lifted her chin until he could see her eyes. They glittered with unshed tears and pain. He sympathized with her. "Everything will work out fine, Lavette. Trust me." He smiled, hoping she would relax a little. She turned her face away, trying to hide her feelings.

"Excuse me, Josiah." Glorianna stood next to him, Kathleen beside her. "Conlon asked that the women leave while the men take care of this situation. We'd like for Lavette to come with us."

Josiah glanced around the room, noting that Glorianna, Kathleen, and Lavette were the only women left in the room besides Mrs. Laughlin, who sat stiff-backed in the chair opposite him. The only men left were Mr. Laughlin and the ones well grounded in Scripture, who could be trusted to look at a situation through God's eyes. He looked back at Glorianna. He didn't want to let Lavette go.

"We'll take good care of her, I promise." Glorianna smiled and stretched out a hand. Josiah nodded and turned back to Lavette.

"You need to leave. Glorianna and Kathleen will be with you until we're done here. I want you to stay with them. Will you?" He waited until Lavette nodded, then gave her a hand up. It took all his willpower not to follow the women from the room so he could accompany Lavette. She looked so vulnerable and alone.

Twenty minutes later, Josiah took a deep breath as he stepped into the kitchen behind the other men. Discipline was never pleasant, but he couldn't fault the way Conlon handled the chore. He'd admonished the Laughlins not only for this occurrence, but for other times they hadn't displayed Christian charity to people who chose to worship with the group. Conlon then reminded them the meetings weren't for perfect people, but for those who wished to worship together because all are sinners. Mrs. Laughlin had turned beet red and exploded. She had the tongue of a shrew and wasn't afraid to use it. She and Lyle had left in a huff, even though they'd been invited to stay for the meal. Josiah had to admit he wasn't sorry to see them leave.

The women were chattering and laughing as they set out the various dishes of food. Josiah's stomach rumbled again, but the general hubbub covered the growl. Lavette sat in a corner of the room with one of the twins on her lap. The other, Andrew, stood beside her, his thumb in his mouth, his gaze fastened on her face. She smiled down at him, looking to Josiah like an angel. Angelina caught one of the loose wisps of Lavette's hair and tugged, pulling the tendril toward her mouth. As Lavette pried open the baby's fist to release her hair, she saw Josiah across the room. The smile she gave him made him wish they were alone. All this time he'd been afraid she would feel abandoned, and here she appeared nearly as comfortable as the other women. What had Glorianna and Kathleen done?

Within a few minutes, the blessing had been said, and people were starting to fill their plates. Josiah wanted to shove everyone aside to get to Lavette. He longed to be with her. He needed to talk to her about what had happened today and why she seemed so at peace when such hurtful things had been said.

He watched as Glorianna took the twins, their faces greasy from the chicken legs clasped in tiny fists. Lavette stood and helped her clean them up. Then Glorianna disappeared with the pair, probably to take them to their room for a nap. Lavette saw him watching her, looked away, then returned his gaze. She smiled again, and Josiah began to work his way through the crowd to her. He couldn't wait any longer.

Standing in front of her at last, he couldn't think of a thing to say. Her cinnamon eyes were wide, the long lashes grazing her cheeks when she blinked. He couldn't stop staring and knew he was making a perfect fool of himself. None of the people in this room would doubt how he felt about Lavette after this. Even he couldn't deny his feelings. He only hoped she had changed her attitude toward God this morning. If she hadn't, it would break his heart to turn away from her.

"You have the most beautiful voice I've ever heard." Josiah could have kicked himself. Why had he opened his mouth and brought up the most painful subject possible? Of course, she wouldn't want to be reminded of that incident so soon after it happened. He wouldn't blame her if she walked away and never spoke to him again.

"Thank you." She gave a shy smile. "I love to sing, and that was my favorite spiritual. I didn't know the other hymns you did earlier, but I'd like to learn."

Josiah tried to make his mouth shut. He knew his jaw had almost hit the floor. She didn't sound upset or angry at all. What had Glorianna done?

"I think I'd like something to eat."

Lavette peeked around him. Most of the others had taken their food outside to where a temporary table was set up. Josiah's stomach gave a low growl. "I guess you'd like some, too." She giggled.

"I've been hungry since I smelled that chicken of yours. I sure hope there's some left. No one knows how to make fried chicken like someone who's raised in the South. My mama grew up there and made the best in the world." He stopped. "At least, she's made the best I tasted so far."

She giggled again. "That's fine. I wouldn't want to make a man doubt his mama's chicken. I believe there's plenty left. Glorianna put the plates over there." She pointed to a spot on the table where two plates waited for them.

Outside, there were two places at the table. Lavette seemed much more comfortable with the others. She even glanced up at the women sometimes when they talked to her. Josiah wanted to ask what had been said before he got to the kitchen, but he didn't quite know how to put it.

The meal wore on, people returning to the kitchen, the men for a second plate of food, then everyone for a piece of pie or cake for dessert. Josiah couldn't keep up with the conversation. He heard bits and pieces about Fort Lowell, the school, the changes needed to the less savory parts of town, and the need for a church with a pastor in residence. Most of the time he simply enjoyed being next to Lavette, watching as she listened to everyone else.

"May I walk you home?" Josiah could smell the hint of cinnamon that seemed to cling to Lavette as if she just stepped out of the kitchen. "That is, if you're ready to leave."

She gazed up at him, her light brown eyes probing. "I should get home. Mrs. Sawyer may be coming back from her daughter's any time, and I'll need to be there. She gets so tired on these long days, but she loves seeing her grandchildren."

He followed her to the kitchen, where she gathered her empty dish and said her good-byes to the women there. On the way from the house, Josiah nodded to Conlon, Quinn, and some of the other men to let them know he was leaving. Taking the cloth-covered bowl from Lavette, Josiah ushered her out into the late afternoon sunshine. A cloudless blue sky stretched overhead. The sun blazed down, not overly hot, but enough to make them willing to stroll rather than rush down the street.

A hummingbird darted past Josiah's ear,

pausing to hover beside a flower long enough to extract a bit of sweetness, then flitting away. The iridescent green of the tiny bird's body gleamed in the sunlight.

"That thing can't be bigger than my hand." Lavette's dulcet tone held a hint of awe.

"They may be small, but I always want to duck when they fly past. The way their wings go so fast makes them sound like a swarm of bees on the attack." Josiah grinned. Lavette's hand tucked in the crook of his arm felt comfortable.

"I'm sorry if I'm nosy, but I have to ask you something."

Lavette studied him, her eyes wide and questioning. "What?"

"When you left the parlor with Glorianna and Kathleen, you looked like the world was coming to an end. Then, when I came in the kitchen, you were smiling and playing with the babies. What happened?" Lavette frowned, and Josiah wondered if he'd overstepped his bounds. "If you don't want to tell, that's fine. I'm curious; that's all."

"I don't mind talking about it. I don't know if I can explain what happened." Lavette slowed, and Josiah matched her pace, waiting for her to continue.

"Glorianna and Kathleen didn't take me to the kitchen where the other women were. Instead, we went to Glorianna's bedroom. We all sat on the bed. I thought they were going to tell me they didn't want me coming around their house anymore."

"They wouldn't do that."

Lavette flashed a smile. "I know that now, but I didn't then."

"So what did they talk about?"

"Well, that's the funny part." Lavette worried her lower lip for a moment. "They didn't talk to me at all. Kathleen started praying, and Glorianna took up when she stopped. I've never heard anyone talk to God like He was standing right next to them. I think Mama may have prayed like that, but only in private."

Josiah bounced on the balls of his feet, trying to be patient. "Did you join in?"

"Not out loud." She shook her head. "No, I don't think I did, but something happened. Between what Conlon said about Joseph forgiving his brothers and these women praying as if they truly cared about me —" She gave Josiah a bewildered look. "I can't explain what happened. One minute, I was afraid and angry, and the next minute this wonderful sense of peace filled me. I don't think I'm mad at God anymore, but I can't tell you why. I'll have to consider this."

They walked in silence. Josiah couldn't believe what she'd said. God was at work in her heart. She might not understand it, but he did. He knew God would work everything out for him and for Lavette. He couldn't recall the last time he'd been so happy.

"Would you like to learn some of the songs we sang this morning?"

She glanced up, her eyes sparkling. "Oh, yes. I liked the one about the fountain. Could you sing it, and I'll try to follow along?"

"That happens to be my favorite hymn." Josiah squeezed his arm closer to his body, pulling Lavette to him. "There is a fountain filled with blood —" By the time he reached the chorus, she'd added her lovely soprano. Her words were hesitant, but Josiah was amazed at how much she'd caught from the singing earlier that morning.

"What beautiful words." Lavette sighed. "I've always loved to sing, but sometimes I'm afraid to."

"Why is that?"

She looked to the side, something in her posture telling him she wasn't comfortable talking about her reason. They turned on the path leading up to Mrs. Sawyer's house. Lavette halted, turning to face Josiah. Her mouth opened, then snapped shut. She stared at the front of his shirt, not looking up at him. Josiah waited, even though he wanted to grab her and make her tell him.

The smell of roasting peppers floated on the breeze. Josiah's stomach rumbled.

Lavette chuckled, a strained sound. She glanced up. "How can you possibly be hungry after all you ate today?"

"Would you believe I'm a growing boy?" Josiah widened his eyes and tried to look forlorn. Lavette laughed.

"No, but I would believe you need a lot of food. I wish I had some more chicken to offer, but I'm afraid it's all gone." She met his gaze. Josiah realized his free hand rested on her shoulder. With only a slight pull, she would be close enough for him to hold her and kiss her. The urge nearly overwhelmed his senses.

A door banged somewhere close. Josiah stepped back. Lavette reached for her dish. Josiah took her elbow in his hand. He turned her toward the house. He'd better get her inside and leave before his emotions took over.

"May I come by in the evenings? I could teach you some more of the songs before next Sunday."

"I haven't sung with anyone in a long time." She looked out at the street, a far-away look in her eyes. "I think I need to, though." She smiled. "I'd be happy to have you come by tomorrow. Do you think we can do the fountain song one more time before you go?"

Josiah followed her example and closed his eyes. He let the words and music wash over him. Their voices seemed to blend in a way few did. He could imagine God in heaven enjoying the words and the sound. Silence hung heavy as the last notes floated away. Clapping startled him. Josiah's eyes flew open. Lavette backed against him. Bertrand Mead stood a few paces away on the path.

"I'm so glad to hear you practicing, my dear. I spoke with Mrs. Sawyer again. I believe she'll be ready to sell me your contract very soon. Then you can perform for me and my patrons."

Chapter 14

The heat from Josiah should have chased away the chill that shook Lavette. Instead, she trembled like a leaf as she huddled next to him. She wondered if the heat came from the force of his anger. He put his arm around her shoulders to protect her from Mead. She could feel the tension in his taut muscles. His fingers dug into her shoulder, yet she drew comfort from the touch.

"You have no hold over Lavette, Mead. Leave her alone."

"Or what?" Mead's lip lifted in an expression of contempt. "You gonna call on your deputy friend to cover for you? There are some things he can't do. When I own Miss Johnson, everything will be legal."

"Mrs. Sawyer won't do that." Lavette's voice shook. "I've been with her for eight years. She can't sell me off like a piece of furniture, especially to someone like you."

"Oh, but that's where you're wrong, my

dear. Your employer is considering staying with her daughter, Gretta, rather than returning home. If she does that, she'll need to get rid of you. Gretta already has help, and with the size of the house, they'll have no room for you."

She would never let someone like you have me. Lavette wanted to scream the words at him, but terror kept her silent. She knew Mead could read the fear in her.

"In case you're wondering, Mrs. Sawyer's son-in-law, Paul, believes me to be a fine, upstanding citizen. You see, he put in a good word with her today. I believe we'll have everything worked out within the next few weeks." He chuckled, and the sound sent a shiver of dread through Lavette. "Keep practicing that singing, my beauty. Soon you'll have an audience who will appreciate your talents."

Mead lifted his hand to touch Lavette's cheek. Josiah caught him by the wrist. His grip must have been tight because a flicker of pain crossed Mead's face. His eyes narrowed.

"Let me go, Boy. This is not your business."

"I believe it is." Josiah moved more in front of Lavette without releasing her or Mead. Mead's expression tensed as if

Josiah were adding more pressure to his arm.

"You don't have any say over what I do here. I'll see to it you regret interfering. Let me go." Mead's voice sounded tight with anger.

With a slight shove, Josiah released the man. Mead stumbled back, then caught himself. He rubbed his wrist, anger giving his face a ruddy tint. "You'll pay for this." He snarled the words, gave Lavette a look that made her skin crawl, and strode past them down the path.

Lavette's heart pounded so hard, she wondered if Josiah could feel the beat. What was happening? Would Mrs. Sawyer sell her contract to Bertrand Mead? Did she intend to live with her daughter instead of returning home?

"You okay?" Josiah's low voice in her ear startled, and comforted, Lavette. This man felt like a solid wall of strength. Somehow, being near him made her feel protected from all the wickedness that could erupt around her.

"I'm fine, just a little shook up." She pushed away from Josiah's warmth. "I need to get inside and see to Mrs. Sawyer."

Josiah guided her to the door, his hand a comforting touch on the small of her back.

"I want to know what your employer has to say about this. I don't understand why Mead thinks he can buy your contract." He studied her, his eyes full of concern. "Right now, I think you're too tired to explain. If you have the time tomorrow, you're welcome to stop by my shop in the afternoon. Usually, business is a little slower then."

She nodded, her throat aching from the tension. "I'll see if can get there." She slipped through the door and listened to his footsteps clump across the porch and recede down the path. *Lord, I don't know what's going on in my life. Something changed in me today. Help me to understand what.* Maybe tomorrow she could bring herself to talk to Josiah about her confusion. Perhaps he could help her understand.

"Lavette, is that you?" Mrs. Sawyer's voice trembled as it did when she was very tired. She'd been gone since early morning. Even if Gretta tried to get her to take a nap, her grandsons were too noisy for her to rest much. Lavette couldn't help wondering how they would manage if Mrs. Sawyer chose to stay here with Paul and Gretta.

"I'm right here. Have you been home long?" Lavette tried to make her voice light so her employer wouldn't guess the turmoil brewing inside. Judging from the lines of exhaustion on Mrs. Sawyer's face, her efforts weren't needed. She appeared to be beyond caring about anything but rest.

The next two hours felt like weeks to Lavette. She hadn't been able to get any information from Mrs. Sawyer before the older woman fell asleep. Lavette worked around the house, catching up on some of the little chores. She wanted to sit and pray or read, but uncertainty kept her from relaxing enough to do that. Where had all the peace gone that she'd felt this morning? Memories of the horror from her childhood rose up to haunt her. Could she share all of her past with Josiah? He was a godly man. Would he turn his back on her when he found out what Miss Susannah's father had done? *Maybe I'm a fool,* she thought, *but I can't see Josiah doing something like that. Lord, help me to trust Josiah with the truth, if that's the right thing to do.*

The tinkling of a bell roused her from her reverie. Mrs. Sawyer was awake. *Oh, please let her tell me what she said to Mr. Mead.* Lavette hurried in to find Mrs. Sawyer struggling to sit up in bed.

"Here, let me help you." She slipped her

arm around the woman's shoulders.

"Thank you, Dear. I get so impatient these days. I want to be able to do everything on my own." Mrs. Sawyer sighed and let Lavette help her dress. "Old age isn't much fun at times, but I wouldn't miss being here and seeing those babies of Gretta's."

"Did you have fun with them today?"

"Oh, my goodness, yes. The boys put on a wild animal show for me." She chuckled. "They read somewhere about a man putting his head in a lion's mouth. Imagine that."

Lavette gasped. "That can't be true. Why would anyone do something so dangerous?"

"Oh, you know these men. Always trying to find something to do that no one else has ever done." Mrs. Sawyer stayed quiet for the walk to the parlor. Lavette put her in the chair by the window and opened the latch to let fresh air inside.

"Marcus was the animal tamer, and Winston and Harold were the beasts." Her eyes crinkled with humor. "Winston growled and acted so fierce. He even tried to bite Marcus a couple of times. I'm afraid Marcus will have to get a friendlier animal to tame."

Lavette couldn't help giggling at the picture of the boys and their show. "I've heard the men who work with wild animals in shows use big whips to control them. I hope Marcus didn't have one of those."

"Oh, no. He wanted to, especially when the tiger tried to bite, but his papa said no. Paul gave the boy a feather and said tickling would be a better torture for his beast. The next thing we knew, all three boys were rolling on the floor, cackling like a bunch of chickens." Her eyes twinkled. "Now, don't you tell those fierce beasts I compared them to something so tame."

"Never." Lavette adjusted a shawl around Mrs. Sawyer's shoulders in case the evening air was too fresh. She tried to keep the strain out of her touch and voice. "You're going to miss that family when we leave."

Mrs. Sawyer tensed. She gestured to a stool on the floor near her. "Sit down, Child." She stayed silent until Lavette was seated. "I'm not sure I'll be going back to Virginia like we planned. Gretta and Paul want me to stay here. Paul seems to think he wouldn't have much trouble making me a small private room at the back of the house."

"But the children. Would you be able to

rest enough with them there?" Lavette didn't want to discourage Mrs. Sawyer from staying with her daughter, but the thought of being sold off terrified her.

"As long as I have a room of my own where I can retreat when the melee gets too intense, I'll be fine." Mrs. Sawyer paused, studying Lavette. "The main problem with my staying here is what to do with you. Gretta has two girls who work for her already, and she doesn't have the room for another. I can't send you back home by yourself."

"Maybe I could share a room with the girls who work for her."

"I'm afraid that would never work. Their room is very small. I've talked to Mr. Mead. Paul knows him. He's a fine, upstanding businessman here in Tucson. He's willing to buy the last two years of your contract. You would work for him for that length of time, then be free to do as you choose."

Bitterness rose like bile in Lavette's throat. She stared at the floor, afraid to look up lest Mrs. Sawyer see the emotion in her eyes. "You can't sell me off." The words came out as a hoarse whisper.

"This man, Mr. Mead, will take good care of you. He's quite a gentleman."

"He's not what you think." Lavette couldn't look up. It took all her willpower to get the words out.

"Are you suggesting Paul doesn't know what he's talking about? He said some good things about Mr. Mead. You would be a great asset to him in his business." Mrs. Sawyer's tone held a note of dismissal. Lavette stood.

"I'll fix you something to eat before you retire." She managed to hold back the tears until she got to the kitchen. There she grabbed a towel, held it over her face, and sobbed. What would become of her? She knew what Mead wanted to happen. Two years with him would be like a lifetime. "What am I to do?" She whispered the question to no one in particular. Josiah's face flashed before her. She could almost hear his low voice and feel the touch of his hand. Tomorrow afternoon while Mrs. Sawyer napped, she would talk with Josiah. Maybe he would understand and have an idea how to help her.

Cottonball clouds dotted a brilliant azure sky as Lavette made her way downtown the next afternoon. Her eyes burned, and her head felt fuzzy from lack of sleep. Every time she'd fallen asleep, she'd dreamed of Mead dragging her off to a noisy saloon where she was forced to sing in front of drunken men who shouted lurid taunts. She would wake covered with sweat, the blanket tangled around her like a shroud, only to fall asleep to a variation of the same dream. Lavette shuddered despite the warmth of the day. Had her dream been a portent of her life to come?

An Indian woman trudged down the street, a *giho* on her back, carrying baskets for sale. A strap running around the woman's forehead held the *giho* in place so the large carrier wouldn't tip as it hung down her back. Lavette had heard about the woven goods the Tohono O'odham Indians sold in Tucson. Their baskets, mats, and sandals were made from desert plants. Gretta had given Lavette one to hold her mending and a larger one for the laundry. Lavette watched as the barefoot woman plodded down the street, her burden swaying with her steps.

The few minutes watching the basket seller helped Lavette forget her destination. Mrs. Sawyer once again sent her to purchase items they needed from the mercantile. Dread tugged at Lavette's feet, moving her slower as she neared the store. What if Mead were there again? What about that awful man from yesterday's meeting? She wiped her clammy hands on her skirts. The mercantile stood across the street, its tall facade staring at her with glass eyes.

She pictured Josiah's big frame and wondered if she could ask him to accompany her on her errands. *No, I can do this. I can't depend on someone else to protect me.* The last time was an accident. Like Mrs. Sawyer said, Mr. Mead is a businessman. He'll be working this afternoon, not engaging in idle conversation here. Lavette squared her shoulders and crossed the street.

The murmuring of men's voices ceased as Lavette stepped inside. After the brightness of the sun, the tomblike darkness blinded her. Her heart thudded. She clutched her bag with the money and the list in fingers that trembled. Hushed whispers began before her vision cleared enough for her to locate the counter. The curtain to the back room fluttered as the man who helped her before strode to the front.

"May I help you?" He smiled and nodded. Lavette forced her feet to carry her forward. She didn't look away from the scarred countertop as she fished the list from her bag.

"We need to have these things, please, Suh." She put the scrap of paper down and watched the man's stained fingers as he picked it up.

"This will only take a minute." The owner must have noticed Lavette's nervous glance at the back of the room. "I won't be leaving the front for this order. You'll be fine. I'll see to it."

Lavette tried to smile. The man's voice sounded vaguely familiar. Her brow tightened as she tried to recall where she'd heard it before. A sudden recollection of the testimonies at the meeting yesterday eased her trepidation. This man had been one of the ones to speak. She hadn't recognized him since he'd been all fixed up then, and here he wore work clothing. She wondered if he was the one who told the truth of what happened between her and Mead here at the mercantile.

Chairs scraped against the floor. Lavette gripped the counter with shaking hands. *Hurry, please hurry.* She could hear footsteps coming her way. She squeezed her eyes shut. *Oh, please don't let Mead be here.*

"Here we go." The owner plunked the items she'd ordered down with a thud that made her jump. "Let me get these

191

wrapped up, and you'll be all ready."

Her fingers shook as she fished some coins out of her reticule. One dropped to the floor and rolled a few feet, coming to rest beside a booted foot. Lavette thought about ignoring the money, but it wasn't hers to waste. She glanced up to see the owner of the boots. Bertrand Mead, a superior smile creasing his face, watched her. Keeping his gaze locked on her, he stooped and picked up the coin. In two steps he stood close enough for her to catch the residue of pipe tobacco clinging to him.

"I believe you dropped something, Miss Johnson." He held out the money. She couldn't move, but only stared at his hand.

The man behind the counter cleared his throat, and Mead tossed the coin down. Within a minute, the owner handed her the change and the package. Lavette moved back toward the door, the parcel clutched tightly to her chest. All noise seemed to be suspended as she fumbled for the latch. A well-manicured hand closed over hers.

"Let me help you with that. I want to speak with Mrs. Sawyer again, so I'll walk you home." Something sinister oozed out in Mead's voice. "We wouldn't want anything to happen to you, would we?"

Chapter 15

Heart pounding, Lavette jerked her fingers from beneath Mead's. The door swung open. She darted out. Behind her she heard the shopkeeper shout something, but she didn't stop. Her slippers made little sound as she hurried away, her ears straining for the sound of footsteps following her.

At the corner, Lavette glanced behind to see Mead standing outside the mercantile watching her. His stance suggested cockiness, making him appear so sure of his hold over her that he didn't need to push. She groaned. A tremor raced through her. Moving out of Mead's sight, Lavette sagged against the wall of a building. The shaded adobe bricks were cool on her back. Sweat-drenched, she welcomed the chill.

A horse whinnied. A freight wagon rumbled past. The vibration in the ground ran up her legs, echoing the quivering in her knees. Her breathing slowed. The moisture on her forehead dried. Relief that she hadn't been followed made Lavette weak. Pushing away from the wall, she glanced back before heading for Josiah's smithy.

A brace of mules dozed in the shade outside Josiah's place. Their tails twitched. Long ears jerked back and forth. Their expressions of utter boredom made them appear to be half-asleep. Flies swooped through the air, buzzing from one beast to the other with an annoying drone.

Josiah stood near the forge, outlined by the glow of the fire. In one hand, he held a pair of tongs, which he used to move an iron bar heating in the coals. Lavette stepped out of the sun into the dimness of the shop. She knew Josiah didn't hear her. Peace seemed to settle over her. Merely being in the presence of this man filled her with a calm she'd never felt before. Her heart ached to be close to him. *Why can't I be free? When so many are able to have freedom, why am I still a slave?* Sorrow welled up inside her. Maybe yesterday slavery hadn't seemed so real, but today she knew she would always live in chains. No matter how she craved what others had, she must learn to live with her lot in life, and Josiah would never be a part of that.

He lifted the iron bar from the coals.

The end glowed white hot. As he swung around, he glanced up and saw her. His face split in a wide grin. She could see the joy sparkling in his eyes. He beckoned her to come inside.

"Afternoon." Josiah's voice rumbled over the whoosh of the bellows as he pulled the cord. "I was beginning to think you might not come."

"I had to wait until Mrs. Sawyer went down for a nap. Then I had some errands to run."

He frowned. "Did you go to the mercantile?" She nodded, and his brow creased further. "Mead is always there this time of day. Did he bother you?"

She looked down, digging her toe into the dirt floor of the smithy. She shrugged. "He didn't follow me today."

"Did he bother you?" Josiah's stern tone made her glance up.

"Not really." She shrugged, unable to meet his gaze. "I think the mercantile owner said something."

Josiah wiped his hands on a rag lying on the bench beside his anvil. In one step, he stood beside her. She could feel the warmth he exuded and the comfort. She wanted to lean toward him, but made her body stay upright and still. Josiah wrapped one of her wiry curls around his finger.

"If you have to go there again, why don't you come here first? I don't mind walking over with you. Mead won't try anything with me around." His dark eyes glittered in the light from the forge. His bulging muscles flexed. Lavette drew in a deep breath, forcing her thoughts away from how wonderful it would feel to have Josiah wrap her in his arms and hold her tight. To her, he represented safety — a safety she would never be able to have.

"What are you making?" She gestured to the hot metal, hoping to distract him from thinking about Mead and her situation. Josiah couldn't do anything about her predicament. No one would be able to help her. Lavette knew she should leave now and not risk losing her heart further to this giant of a man, but like a moth drawn to a flame, she couldn't go.

"I'm working on some shoes for those mules. One of them has a peculiar hoof and needs a special fit. He went lame when he was shod poorly. I've been trying to adjust the shoes, and he's doing better."

The mules being talked about still stood in sleepy ignorance outside the smithy, the twitching of their long ears the only indication they were awake.

"I remember Papa talking about one of the blacksmiths at Wild Oaks who didn't do his work right. I never quite understood what Papa meant, but he said the wrong fit could ruin a horse."

"That's right." Josiah pulled a stool close enough to the bench so they could talk and she could see, but far enough to be away from the danger of flying sparks. "Here, sit down. I need to work on this shoe so I can finish by the time Mr. Hernandez returns." Josiah picked up the iron bar with a shorter pair of tongs, frowned at the red-orange glow of the heated portion, and thrust it back into the coals.

"I'm sorry to interrupt your work. Did that cool off too much?"

"Yep. In order to work it the way I need to, the metal has to be white hot. Otherwise it won't bend or flatten properly." Josiah strode across the shop and picked up a packing crate with one meaty hand. Placing the wooden box beside Lavette's stool, he sat down, the lower crate putting him eye to eye with her.

"While we're waiting for that bar to reheat, I want to hear about your talk with Mrs. Sawyer." His gaze bored into her, making her want to squirm. She felt like she'd been hiding something from him. "I want to know why Mead thinks he has a hold over you. What did he mean about owning you?"

Lavette fidgeted with the string around the package from the mercantile, which she held in her lap. Josiah extracted the parcel and set it up on a bench lined with rows of tools. He took her hands in his, bringing warmth to her cool fingers.

"Lavette, I don't know how you feel, but I care for you a lot. I've never felt this way about anyone before. If there's any way possible, I want to help you."

Her breath caught as she saw the look in his eyes. He cared for her as much as she cared for him. Was this love? She hesitated to give the emotion a name, not wanting to admit the depth of her feelings.

"I told you about the contract Mrs. Sawyer has on me." She paused as Josiah nodded. "Well, she's considering staying in Tucson with her daughter and son-in-law. They have no room for me, so she's thinking of selling the remainder of my contract. Paul is the one who recommended Mr. Mead." Lavette's throat ached with the need to cry. "After talking with Mrs. Sawyer, I can't see any way you can help me. Soon I'll belong to Mr. Mead, and he can do with me as he pleases."

"What about us?" Josiah's hands tightened on hers.

"There is no us. There never can be." Bitterness made her spit out the words.

"Do you care for me?"

"What does it matter?" She couldn't meet Josiah's gaze.

"It matters to me. Do you care for me?" The heat of his gaze drilled into her. She wanted to deny her feelings for him. All she had to do was to say she felt nothing, then he would leave her alone and be safe. If she admitted her feelings, Josiah might do something foolish that would only end up hurting him. She would never be free, and he had to understand that.

"You are special to me. A friend." *Coward!* She berated herself. "Josiah, don't worry about me. You know what it's like to be a slave. We have no choice in this."

Holding Lavette's small hands in his, Josiah stared at the contrast between his dark coffee skin and her lighter, milkier tones. Her fine bones gave her a delicate appearance, while his large frame sometimes made him feel like a lumbering bear. Right now, he felt as stupid as an animal. He didn't know what to say to her. Lavette

199

seemed to be shutting him out when she needed him most. He knew she cared for him. When she looked at him wide-eyed, the longing and love shone like a lantern on a dark night. Being a friend wasn't what he wanted anymore, and he was sure friendship wasn't what God wanted for them.

"Don't you remember the story of Joseph? Conlon talked about it yesterday — how Joseph's brother sold him into slavery and all the bad things that happened, but God was there watching over him. God made good things happen."

Lavette sat back, tugging at her hands. "God doesn't care whether I'm a bond-woman or free. I can't count on Him for anything."

"But, yesterday —" Josiah was stunned.

"Yesterday I felt a measure of peace, that's true. I've thought about it, though. What I felt was because I was with a bunch of folks who've never been enslaved. They don't understand the horror like you and I do."

He knew he had to set her straight, yet he hesitated. Would she equate him with all the others who'd been at the meeting? "Lavette, I've never been a slave."

"What?" She drew back again, her eyes

going wide. "But you're black, and the war only ended nine years ago. How could you not have been a slave?"

"My father and mother were slaves. Right after they were married, their master's son, Edward, decided to move north. He didn't like slavery, didn't agree that it was right. His father let him choose two slaves to take with him to care for his needs. He chose my parents. After they were settled in New York, he gave my parents their freedom. I was born six months later to emancipated parents and have always been free." He smiled. "At least in that sense. I wanted to talk to you about the other kind of slavery, spiritual bondage."

"I don't want to hear any more." Lavette jerked her hands free. "No wonder you don't understand what I'm going through. You've never been there. You're no better than one of them." She jumped to her feet.

"Lavette, no." Josiah reached for her. Tears filled her eyes. She turned away, rushing for the door. "Wait."

Feeling helpless, Josiah watched as the girl of his dreams raced away from him. What now? How could he make her trust him again? *Oh, Lord, what have I done?* Head bowed and shoulders slumped,

Josiah tried to think of a way to explain things to Lavette. His gaze fell on the parcel from the mercantile that she'd left lying on his tool bench. He touched the wrap with a finger, feeling the paper crinkle in the indention.

A bray from outside startled him. He'd forgotten the mules. Mr. Hernandez would be here shortly and expect his animals to be ready. Glancing at the forge, Josiah could see the iron bar glowing white in the coals. He picked up the tongs and drew the rod out. He would finish the shoes, then take the package to Lavette. By that time, maybe she would have calmed down and they could talk. She had to understand. Perhaps if he admitted his love to her, she would accept his help. There had to be a way to keep her away from Mead.

An hour later, Josiah strode down the street. Mr. Hernandez had taken longer than he thought to return for the mules. Waiting had proved impossible. All Josiah wanted to do was see Lavette again. At least no one else had shown up with more work. One good thing came of the waiting. He had a plan he thought might work. He only hoped Lavette agreed with it.

The sun was dipping toward the western mountains as Josiah hurried up the path leading to Mrs. Sawyer's house. The porch boards creaked under his weight. He sniffed, wondering at the lack of supper smells in the air. Usually, he could at least enjoy the scent of Lavette's cooking. His mouth watered at the thought.

Knocking on the door, Josiah began to shift from one foot to another as he waited. Where was she? The faint ding of a bell came from inside. He frowned. Hadn't Lavette once mentioned Mrs. Sawyer calling to her by ringing a bell? Quiet enveloped him. He couldn't hear talking or footsteps.

Josiah stepped off the porch and started around the house to see if Lavette was in the backyard. Perhaps she was taking down some laundry and hadn't heard anything.

"Help me."

The words drifted out of one of the side windows where Josiah assumed the bedrooms were. He turned and ran back to the front door and lifted the latch. Pushing the portal open he called, "Hello, anybody home?"

"Help." Once more the shaky voice cried out. Josiah rushed in, following the sound. Mrs. Sawyer lay beside her bed, the covers tangled around her legs, a small bell clutched in one hand. Josiah eased her up enough to loosen the blankets, then lifted her gently into the bed.

"What happened? Where's Lavette?"

Mrs. Sawyer closed her eyes, tears tracing a track down her wrinkled cheeks. "I sent her to town for some things while I napped. When I woke, she wasn't here. I've called and called." A hiccuping sob shook her. "I tried to get up myself and fell."

"You mean Lavette hasn't come home yet? She left my place over an hour ago and was headed here." Josiah paused. He'd assumed Lavette was going straight home. Where else would she go?

"When I first awakened, that nice Mr. Mead stopped by. I hadn't fallen then. He promised to find Lavette and see that she came home."

A chill raced through Josiah. Mead was looking for Lavette? He didn't want to think of what could have happened.

"I'll go fetch someone to help you, Ma'am." Josiah crossed the room before stopping to look back. "As soon as I do, I'll go find Lavette. I'll see to it that she's safe."

The front door slammed hard enough to rattle the whole house as Josiah rushed out. He ran all the way to the Sullivans' and banged on the door. Concern wiped away Glorianna's smile as she looked at him.

"Josiah, what's happened?"

"Lavette is missing. Mrs. Sawyer needs help. Can you go or send someone to help her while I look for Lavette?"

Glorianna barely had time to nod her head before he raced away. Where should he start looking? As he neared town, he could hear the faint sounds of revelry. The saloon. If Mead found her, he would take her there. As his footsteps turned toward the seedy establishment, Josiah didn't want to think what Mead would do once he had Lavette in his grasp.

Chapter 16

Raucous laughter and the tinny plink of piano keys jarred Lavette's already-frayed nerves. Cigarette and cigar smoke hung like a pall in the air. Two women, their lips and cheeks brightened unnaturally, sauntered about the room, hips swaying in a saucy rhythm. Lavette cringed, trying to draw away from the nauseating scene.

"I knew you would warm to me." Mead's breath brushed the hair by her ear. Lavette tried to pull away. His grip tightened. "What's the matter? Think you're too good for a place like this?"

"Please, I need to get home." Lavette could imagine the malevolence in Mead's eyes. The man had no heart or conscience. "My mistress will be expecting me."

"Oh, that is true." He seemed to be mocking her. "I visited with dear Mrs. Sawyer, Amelia, a short time ago. I promised I would find you and get you home."

He gave a wicked chuckle. "Of course, I didn't say how soon I would return you."

"But, she'll need help getting up from bed." Panic rushed through Lavette at the thought of the partially invalid woman trying to do things on her own and getting hurt. She jerked again, and Mead switched his hold, hitting a nerve that sent a painful tingle down her arm, numbing her fingers.

"The old biddy will have to manage. I brought you here so you could see where you'll be working." He gestured across the room with his free hand at the small platform with curtains around the back. "There's where you'll be performing for the crowds."

Fear caught in her throat. The sharp scent of beer, along with the variety of noises and sounds, brought back too many memories. She could almost feel Miss Susannah's father standing behind her. She tried to glance around, but Mead's gaze caught hers. He pulled her closer. The cacophony in the background faded as terror gripped her.

"Of course, I'll be expecting a private performance." His beady eyes were filled with knowledge and lasciviousness. Turning her head, Lavette tried to remind herself that she was a slave and nothing could be done about that. Josiah's face swam before her. *No, I can't think of you, Josiah, or I'll never be able to live my life in peace. I've got to give you up.* Agony tore through her at the thought.

"Come along, my dear. You'll be the hit of the show, so to speak." Mead began to drag her across the floor. Conversation halted. Men turned to stare. Muttered conversation fluttered about the room as she and Mead passed.

"You see, my sweet, they're all amazed by your beauty, and they haven't even heard your voice. I, at least, already knew of your dulcet tones before I found you here."

Lavette stopped. She couldn't breathe as she took in the implications of what he'd said.

Lifting her arm, Mead forced her to go up the steps to the stage. She felt the patrons' eyes were boring holes in her back. Her stomach burned. She took shallow breaths to fight the nausea threatening her.

"You're surprised that I knew of you." Mead pressed her against his side, his mouth next to her ear. "You see, I was there when you sang as a young girl."

Lavette's heart pounded. Blackness seeped across her vision. He couldn't have been there. He couldn't know her shame.

"I visited a neighboring plantation, a distant relative. This gentleman took me to hear the girl with the marvelous voice." Mead's breath smelled of beer and cigarettes, but Lavette couldn't turn away. "I loved your voice, my sweet, but I wasn't blind. Even though you were so young, I could see the potential beauty you would become. Imagine my delight when I heard you singing in the backyard of Mrs. Sawyer's house. I knew at that moment you would be mine."

"Please don't make me do this."

"Oh, but the men want to hear you. I've told them all about how you sing. They've been clamoring for you. See how quiet they are?"

She didn't think her legs would hold her up any longer. They shook worse than a leaf in the fall wind. Lavette gripped the sides of her skirt, clenching the material tight, trying to draw strength from the fabric.

"You may think you can beat me, my sweet." Mead's thumb rubbed the outside of her arm in a way that sent a wash of revulsion through Lavette. "If you can't bring yourself to sing today, then perhaps we can go straight to the private performance for me. I'll be happy to show you to my room."

"No." Lavette gasped. The subdued noise in the room bothered her more than the din when they first entered. She felt every man in the saloon watching and listening to what Mead was saying to her.

"Ready?" She could hear the triumph in his voice and looked up. He smirked at her. He knew she wouldn't be able to do anything other than what he asked.

"I can't think of anything to sing."

"I'm sure you remember some of the music you learned as a child."

Her face warmed. She'd all but forgotten those horrible ditties she'd been forced to sing. At that age, she hadn't understood the bawdiness of the lyrics. Even now, she didn't fully understand, not did she want to.

"That was so long ago." She hoped he'd think she didn't recall them.

"I could join you. The men would love that — unless you can think of something else to perform."

She nodded. Mead released her arm, turned her to face the crowd, and stepped to one side. Lavette opened her mouth. Nothing came out. She'd never been this frightened. *Oh, God, did Joseph have to*

210

do things like this when he was a slave?

"Sing now, or you'll regret your silence." Mead's low-voiced threat startled her, and a song popped into her mind.

The saloon doors swung open, but she didn't look up. Lavette closed her eyes and began to sing. Utter quiet enveloped the crowd. As she moved into the refrain, she could feel Mead near her, his anger a palpable thing. At the end of the chorus, she stopped. She only knew the one verse and wasn't sure what to do now. Applause and cheers broke out from the patrons. Mead's fingers clenched on her arm, then eased.

"Only that voice saved you. If they had booed instead of cheering —"

"I believe we'll show the lady out now, Mr. Mead."

Lavette almost collapsed at the sound of Josiah's voice. He stood at the edge of the platform, his face a study in conflicting emotions. When he looked at Mead, she saw the anger held on a tight rein. When he looked at her, she could see concern and love. Behind Josiah stood Quinn, his hand resting on the butt of his pistol.

Mead's fingers dug deep into the flesh of her arm. Lavette gasped.

"The young lady was entertaining the boys. I'm sure she didn't mind." Mead gave them a contemptuous smile.

"Now that she's done, why don't you let Josiah walk her home?" Quinn took a step closer.

Mead released her arm. Lavette started to move to the steps, but Josiah reached up, grasped her waist, and swung her down beside him. Although his huge hands were gentle, she couldn't help wincing when he bumped the arm Mead had abused. Josiah seemed to notice and took care to stay away from that side. He slipped an arm around her shoulders, pulling her close to him as he led her out of the saloon.

She didn't know which helped the most, the warmth of the day or the warmth coming from Josiah, but the chill began to fade as they walked away from the downtown area. Quinn strode beside them, his hand still hovering near his gun. Lavette understood Josiah's wisdom in bringing the lawman to the saloon with him. On his own, Josiah wouldn't have had the power to get her out of there without a fight.

"I must say I've never heard that song sung better or in a place that needed it more." Quinn began to chuckle. "Did you see the look on Mead's face, Josiah?"

A low rumble began in Josiah's chest. He still had his arm around her, and Lavette could feel the vibrations. "As my mama would say, 'You could have knocked him over with a feather.' I think I should teach Lavette the other stanzas, and she can sing for them on a regular basis." Josiah and Quinn both laughed, although the sound still held a note of tension. "What made you sing that anyway?" Josiah gave her shoulder a light squeeze.

"I couldn't think of any songs. He threatened me with — with — Anyway, I asked God if Joseph ever had to face anything like this, and then that hymn popped into my head."

"I'm heading back to the office before I have to get home." Quinn waved at them and turned down the next street.

"Mrs. Sawyer." Now that the ordeal was over, exhaustion made Lavette feel weak. She wasn't sure she could walk home, let alone do all her chores when she arrived.

"Don't worry about her." Josiah took his arm from around her. His large fingers wrapped around hers, and he slowed his stride so she didn't have to walk so fast. "Glorianna was going to go over or send her helper, Alicia, to see to Mrs. Sawyer. The lady will be well taken care of.

"You see how amazing God is?" Josiah's eyes twinkled in the waning light. "You didn't ask Him for help, but He gave you the right song to sing. I'll bet most of those men have never heard that one before."

"The fountain hymn was all that came to mind." Lavette agreed with Josiah on the wonder of it. "You'll have to teach me the other verses sometime." He began to sing and she joined him.

"There is a fountain filled with blood —"

Lavette hummed softly as she sorted beans. Last night she thought she would never be rested again. After her ordeal at the saloon, she'd come home to find Glorianna and the twins entertaining Mrs. Sawyer. Josiah told her about her employer's fall from bed. He also said he would get Conlon to speak with Paul Ashton about Mead. Josiah suggested maybe something else could be worked out, but he wouldn't say what. Lavette had gone to bed early and awakened with the dawn, surprised she hadn't been plagued by nightmares.

A gentle knock rattled the kitchen door. Lavette hurried to open it. Glorianna stood there, a book in one hand. She smiled.

"Come in." Lavette held the door open. "What have you done with Angelina and Andrew?"

"Shame on me, I left them home taking a nap." Glorianna grinned. "They wouldn't like it if they knew where I was. Those two adore you."

"They are sweet." Lavette smiled as Glorianna snorted. "They remind me of my youngest sister when she was a baby. She was as ornery as the day is long, but she was so cute, you couldn't stay mad at her. When she looked at me with those wide brown eyes and that puppy dog expression, I'd melt inside. I'm afraid we spoiled her."

Glorianna chuckled. "I can understand that. Among Conlon and me, Quinn and Kathleen, and everyone else we know, the twins don't stand a chance." She handed the book to Lavette. "I brought you this Bible." She looked down, seeming uncertain. "When I started out, I thought this was a grand idea. Then I realized that most of the people who were slaves couldn't read. I don't mean to insult you."

"A Bible." Lavette ran her hand over the cover. She hesitated. Somehow, she knew she could trust Glorianna with the truth. "I do know how to read. I grew up as the playmate to the master's daughter. I had to be with her all day and sometimes at night. Her father had a tutor for her even though

215

Miss Susannah hated learning. I soaked up all her lessons like a sponge. Miss Susannah had to repeat everything so many times, I couldn't help but learn."

Glorianna laughed. "I'm glad to hear that. Did you learn sums, too?"

"Yes. I'm one of the few blacks who are educated. I did teach my family a little. On the nights when I was allowed to go home, they had me spend hours showing them figures or teaching them the letters. We had to be careful not to let anyone know, though."

"That's wonderful." Glorianna tapped the Bible. "I thought you might like to read the story of Joseph for yourself. Have you ever read the Bible?"

"No, Ma'am. I've never even held one before."

"The story of Joseph is found in the very first book of the Bible, Genesis." Glorianna took the book and riffled through the pages. "Here you go. This is the part about Joseph, although you might want to start at the beginning and read what happened before then."

Lavette accepted the Bible and hugged it. "I can't wait." She bit her lip, wondering if she could ask Glorianna what was on her heart. This had been bothering her most of the day, and she needed to talk to someone.

"What is it?"

Lavette jumped. Had Glorianna known her thoughts?

"You look like you wanted to ask me something." Glorianna chuckled. "Don't look so guilty."

Looking down, Lavette sighed and hoped this would be the right thing to do. "I do have a question."

"Yes?"

"I've been angry and bitter at God for a long time. Then last Sunday at your house I felt such a peace after you and Kathleen prayed. I thought all those old feelings would be gone." Lavette stopped, unsure how to continue.

"Then the old bitterness popped up again, and you're wondering if you really felt God's peace or not, right?"

Lavette's mouth fell open. "How did you know?"

Glorianna patted Lavette's arm. "We all have doubts about our walk with God. That's one of the reasons we need to meet together. As Christians, we can encourage one another. When we are alone too long, then it's easy to doubt ourselves or God."

"But what do I do about these feelings?"

"Pray." Glorianna smiled. "It's so simple, yet we often forget. Prayer is the best remedy for fears, uncertainty, or a lack of faith." She pursed her lips in thought. "Did you ever pull a weed, only to have the root break off, and before you knew it, another weed sprang up?"

Lavette nodded.

"Bitterness can be like that weed. We may get the main part of the plant pulled up the first time, but there are still all the little roots that can send up shoots at unexpected times. When they do, don't panic. Pray."

A few minutes later, Glorianna left. Lavette turned to the story of Joseph, wondering what else this man faced while a slave. Had God helped him through the hard times?

Chapter 17

Josiah turned from the anvil to the bench with his tools lined in neat rows. He frowned. "What is wrong with me lately?"

"I don't think I have time to list everything that's wrong with you."

Startled, Josiah tried to act indifferent. He hadn't seen Conlon enter the smithy. Focused on the job at hand and the problems with Lavette and Mead, he hadn't heard a thing. He flashed a grin at his friend. "You'd better not start, or I might be tempted to put your horse's shoes on upside down the next time."

"Threats. I never thought you'd stoop so low, Josiah." Conlon shook his head and sighed. "It's amazing what love will do to a man." He chuckled. "Now, tell me what's wrong."

Josiah gestured at the tool-laden table. "I can't seem to find the piece I need. I always put things in the same spot, but now

I need my creaser for this shoe, and it's not there."

"Hmm." Conlon rubbed his chin and peered at the variety of blacksmith implements. His eyes sparkled. "I don't suppose what you're looking for could be in your hand, could it?"

Heat warmed his face as Josiah stared at the creaser in his hand. Conlon gave a guffaw that the whole neighborhood could have heard. Shaking his head, Josiah sighed and gave a sheepish grin. "I don't suppose you'd believe I was trying to see if you knew what a creaser was?"

"Nope. I remember acting like a fool when I met Glory. I'm kind of enjoying seeing you do the same." Conlon smirked. "As I recall, you weren't too sympathetic with me then."

"Hey, what happened to helping a brother?"

"I helped you. I told you exactly where to find what you'd lost."

Josiah groaned. "I give up. Have some coffee while I finish this job. Then we can talk."

Picking up a hammer, Josiah set the creaser along the side of the hot horseshoe. With a few strokes, he made the creases the nails would fit in. Taking up the punch, he made the holes he needed inside the crease, careful to not damage the surface of his anvil. When he finished the last nail hole, he placed the finished shoe to one side to cool while he put his tools away.

"Did you get them all in the right place?" Conlon pretended to examine the tool bench. "I wouldn't want to have to come by every day to show you where everything is."

Josiah slapped his friend on the shoulder, slopping Conlon's coffee over the rim of the mug. Conlon moved the cup to the side to keep the liquid from spilling on his uniform.

"I think you're having trouble taking a joke right now." Conlon wiped the drips from the bottom of the cup and shook his finger. "Glory said you came by to see me this morning. I thought I'd see what you wanted. Maybe I should have stayed away."

Josiah filled his mug with coffee that looked more like sludge than drinkable brew. He tried to look serious. "I guess you're right. I'm as touchy as a bear right out of hibernation."

"Is this a roundabout way of asking for food? That's what those bears always want."

Josiah groaned and shook his head.

Conlon gave him a wicked grin. Taking a sip of the scalding coffee, Josiah grimaced. "I don't know why I keep drinking this stuff. I think this could eat the nail holes through those horseshoes."

"I have to agree. Is this the same pot we shared two weeks ago, or have you considered making some fresh?"

"I usually make it fresh every morning, although the way my mind is working lately, this could be from two weeks ago." Josiah took another slug. "I wanted to talk to you about one of your men."

Conlon straightened. His expression changed from joking to serious. "Is something wrong?"

"No, not wrong, so to speak." Josiah rubbed the back of his neck. "It's Paul Ashton. Do you know him well?"

"We aren't close, but he's one of my men." Conlon's brows drew together even farther. "He's the son-in-law of the woman Lavette works for."

Putting his cup down, Josiah rubbed his palms on the legs of his pants. "I don't know if you're aware of what Mrs. Sawyer, Lavette's employer, is planning to do." When Conlon shook his head, Josiah continued. "She plans to stay in Tucson with the Ashtons rather than returning home."

"That's good news, isn't it?" Conlon looked puzzled.

"In a way, yes. The problem is she can't keep Lavette. Paul recommended she sell the remainder of Lavette's contract to Bertrand Mead. He says Mead is a fine, upstanding citizen, and Mrs. Sawyer believes him."

"Has she met Mead?"

"Yep. He's put on such an act that she talks like he's a saint or something."

"So what can I do?" Conlon rested against the side of the tool bench, placing his empty cup beside him.

"I thought maybe you could talk to Ashton. Does he know Mead well? If not, maybe he would see him in a different light."

Conlon lifted off his cap and ran a hand through his hair. "Unfortunately, Paul may not be swayed. For some reason, he spends a lot of his time off in the saloon. I think he knows exactly what kind of person Mead is. In fact, my guess would be that he's doing this at Mead's bidding."

Josiah felt as if someone had knocked the air out of him. He'd counted on Paul Ashton's help. Now what would he do?

"I'll try to talk to him anyway, but don't count on it doing much good. Has Lavette spoken with Mrs. Sawyer about Mead?"

"She tried, but Mead can put on a good act. Mrs. Sawyer won't believe anything bad about him because she hasn't seen that side of him."

"Well, I've got to get back out to the fort." Conlon straightened and slapped his cap on his head. "I'll try talking to Paul." Josiah followed Conlon outside. Conlon swung up on the horse, then paused. "You know, I wish Glory and I had the money. We would go buy Lavette's contract and release her." He shook his head and reined his horse around.

Stunned, Josiah stood where he was watching the dust billow up around Conlon's horse's legs as they trotted off. Why hadn't he thought of that? *Lord, am I stupid? This is the answer, and I didn't see it.* Josiah rushed around the side of the smithy to the rooms at the back where he lived. Dropping onto his knees, he felt for the loose board beside his bed. With a pro-testing creak, the board lifted, revealing a box in the crevice below.

His fingers trembled as Josiah shook out the coins he'd saved. They fell with a mu-sical clink on his blanket. His heart sank. This was a paltry amount. He had no idea how much Mead was willing to pay or how much Mrs. Sawyer wanted for Lavette's contract, but he knew his savings weren't enough. Scraping the coins back into the bag, he hid them once more. Excitement made his movements jerky. He had a plan now, and this afternoon he would begin to put it into action.

The comforting melody of Josiah's song floated around her as Lavette took the dry clothes from the line and folded them in the basket. She'd come to think of the fountain hymn as Josiah's song because he taught it to her and loved the words so much. All day she couldn't seem to get the tune out of her head. After last night, she thought she would never sing again, let alone this song. For some reason, though, her heart wasn't weighed down with fear and trepidation over what the future held. Something in her was changing.

This morning she'd tried once again to talk to Mrs. Sawyer about Bertrand Mead. Lavette wanted to tell her mistress what happened yesterday at the saloon, but Mrs. Sawyer refused to hear any of it, saying she wouldn't have such a fine gentleman's character maligned. Lavette knew it wasn't her place to push the point. She'd learned long ago, the hard way, that people weren't interested in her thoughts on anything. Speaking up only brought pain.

Instead of arguing, she'd gone to her room for a few minutes to read more of Joseph's story. She took comfort in the fact that Joseph, despite being chosen by God, had to suffer the same as she and her people had to suffer. Joseph didn't seem to have any resentment to deal with like she did. Perhaps she hadn't given God the chance to work in her life. Lavette frowned, and the melody faltered. Her opinion of God was faltering right now. She didn't know what way to turn sometimes.

"I was getting ready to join you. Don't stop."

Lavette screeched and clutched the sheet she was folding. Whirling around, she faced Josiah. How he'd managed to get so close without her hearing him, she didn't know.

"I didn't mean to scare you."

She folded the cloth, put it on the full basket, and glared at him. "I'm not sure I believe that. My brother used to sneak up on me. He had that same grin on his face when I screamed."

Josiah stepped closer. His gaze held hers. She wanted to grab another sheet off the line and hide behind it. This man set her

226

heart pounding so loud, she couldn't think. He lifted a lock of her hair that had escaped the bun at the nape of her neck, and the strand curled around his finger like it belonged there. He tugged. She took a step closer, tilting her head back to still meet his gaze. His huge hand covered her cheek. She closed her eyes and leaned into the touch. A sigh of contentment escaped to dance on the breeze.

The warm touch of his lips on hers surprised her, then stole her breath away. She'd never been kissed like this before. The only kisses she'd known were the ones forced on her when she'd been a slave at Wild Oaks. Those had been hard, mean, and hurtful — nothing at all like Josiah's kiss. This one could go on forever, and she wouldn't mind.

He encircled her with his massive arms, his touch so gentle. Releasing her mouth, Josiah held her close, his breath warm on her forehead. She rested her cheek against his chest. He smelled of soap, smoke, and the faint scent of sweat.

"That's what I wanted to know." The rumble of his voice wrapped around her.

"What's that?"

"I needed to know how you felt about me." His answer surprised her. She arched back to look at him. He smiled. "I know how I feel about you, Lavette. I love you. Before I put my plan into action, I had to know if you felt something for me too."

She pushed away from him. Love? This gentle giant of a man loved her? Panic grabbed her. She couldn't let this happen. She had to keep him at a distance. Inside she knew it was too late. He'd stolen her heart long ago.

"I can't love you." She ached as she spoke. "This will never work. You have to leave and forget me."

He reached out, and she moved farther away. "Do you love me, Lavette?"

"I can't. You don't know what I've done."

"Then tell me. I can't imagine you doing anything wrong."

Panic and horror closed around her. "I had no choice. When I was at Wild Oaks — in the early years of the war —"

Josiah lifted her hand and kissed her fingers. "You didn't have a choice when you were there. You had to do what your owner told you to do."

"He used to touch me." Her voice broke.

"Oh, Sweetheart." Josiah pulled her into his arms again. "I know the horrible things women had to do. My mother was forced to do them. That's one of the reasons Mr. Bellingham chose my father and mother to take with him when he went north. He wanted to get my mother away from his brothers." He stroked a hand over her hair. "That's over. All I care about now is if you love me."

"Oh, Josiah."

"Do you?"

She glanced around the yard, feeling an urgency to escape. She couldn't lie to him. Looking up, she saw the anguish in his eyes. "Yes." The word tore from her. Tears filled her eyes. "I love you so much, but I can't let this happen. I'm not free to care that much for anyone."

Josiah glowed. Before she could react, he grabbed her and hugged her to him once more. This time his kiss wasn't as gentle. This kiss claimed her as his. She didn't fight him. She wanted to be his. He set her back on her feet. A silly grin creased his cheeks. She laughed, unable to remember when she'd felt so giddy.

"I need to talk to Mrs. Sawyer. Is she awake?"

Lavette shook her head, uncertain whether she could speak yet.

"When will she be ready for company?"

"I — uh." Lavette stiffened as Josiah

grinned wider. His smug look said he knew exactly why she couldn't put a thought together. She smiled and shook her head at him. He was right. His kisses had chased away all her sensibility.

"Let me gather this laundry and we'll go in. If you'd like, I have some pie and coffee. Mrs. Sawyer should be awake soon."

"Let me carry this." Josiah picked up the heavy basket as if it weighed nothing. Leading the way across the yard, Lavette remembered her morning's discovery. At the time, she'd wanted to share the news with Josiah. Now, she wasn't certain of his reaction. She whirled around, almost knocking the laundry from his arms.

"I about forgot to tell you, I think I know what to do about Mr. Mead." Josiah's eyebrows lifted, and she hurried on. "Glorianna brought me a Bible. I was reading about Joseph. Anyway, I read what happened with Potiphar's wife. She tried to do to Joseph what Mr. Mead wants to do to me."

Josiah nodded. "And?"

"Don't you see? Joseph ran away. I can run away from here. Maybe I can hide somewhere, and you can come later." Her voice died away. This had sounded so good when she'd thought of it, but as she put the plan into words, she could see the difficulties involved. How would she escape when she had so little money? Where would she go?

"Lavette, Joseph ran away from the sinful act. He didn't try to escape from his responsibilities. Running away never works. Joseph stayed and faced his troubles. Yes, he spent time in prison, but he trusted God to work everything out, and He did."

"But I don't know if I have that kind of faith. I have doubts that God can work this out. I'm scared." Her voice fell to a whisper.

Josiah set the basket on the ground and pulled her into his embrace once more. Her tears wet his shirt, but he didn't seem to mind. She felt the gentle touch of his lips on her forehead. Peace stole over her. Josiah had such a strong faith. Could she trust Jesus as all her new friends suggested? She wiped her eyes and stepped back,

"I'm sorry. Sometimes I don't think things through."

"We're all that way." Josiah picked up the laundry. His stomach growled. "I believe I heard something about pie?"

She sniffed and gave a light laugh. "I

hope I have enough. From the sound of things, you could eat the whole thing. By the way, why did you want to see Mrs. Sawyer?"

Josiah gave her a wide grin. "Because I have a plan to rescue a damsel in distress."

"What? You didn't tell me." Lavette hopped up the steps to open the door. "What is it?"

Josiah stopped to give her a peck on the cheek. "It's a surprise. You'll find out after Mrs. Sawyer agrees with me."

Chapter 18

Lavette danced on pins and needles, waiting for the ding of Mrs. Sawyer's bell. Josiah refused to say more. He ate two pieces of pie and drank his coffee, acting like he didn't have a care in the world. If he wasn't so big, she would pick him up and shake him. He kept saying to be patient, but the anticipation wouldn't let her.

She stirred the coals to life in the stove. The door screeched like a cat with its tail stepped on. Josiah's chuckle brought her around.

"What are you laughing about now?"

"You."

"Me?" She placed her hands on her hips in exasperation. "Why?"

"Because you've been waiting for something, and now you've missed it."

She wanted to stuff her apron in his mouth. At the same time, his lightness of attitude made her long to join him. A bell dinged. She gaped.

"Is that what you're meaning? Did she already ring the bell once?"

He nodded. Lavette gave him a withering glare before starting to stalk out of the room. Josiah grabbed her hand and pulled her onto his lap. His huge hand cupped her cheek, turning her to look at him.

"You aren't really mad, are you?"

"Of course I am." She crossed her arms and huffed. Her mouth twitched, and he grinned. He gave her a quick kiss and lifted her back onto her feet.

"I'll wait until you have her up and ready for company."

Lavette sped down the hall. She had to be careful, or she would be in such a hurry, she would jerk Mrs. Sawyer out of bed, throw her clothes on her, and rush her into the parlor to hear what Josiah had to say.

"Good afternoon, Ma'am. Did you have a good nap?"

"Yes, I did." Mrs. Sawyer's brow wrinkled, "I thought I heard voices. Is someone here?"

"Yes, Ma'am." Lavette lifted her mistress into a sitting position and began to help her dress. "My friend, Josiah, is here. He'd like to speak with you when you're ready."

"Why certainly, although I was hoping

Mr. Mead had stopped by. He's such a charming sort." She chuckled. "If I were years younger, I believe I might be taken with the man."

Lavette bit back a groan. She picked up the brush and began to straighten Mrs. Sawyer's hair. How could this woman be so deceived? The man must have missed his calling as an actor in one of those fancy theaters back East. He certainly could cover up his true self.

"There we go." Lavette placed the brush back on the shelf, hoping Mrs. Sawyer didn't notice her impatience. "Are you ready to go out to the parlor? The weather outside is beautiful. I already have the window open, and you can hear the birds singing."

"That sounds wonderful." Mrs. Sawyer eased up with Lavette's help and began to shuffle down the hallway. "I think I'm still a little tired from my visit to Gretta. I don't believe I'll move in with them until Paul has my room done. Those grandchildren are fun, but they wear a person down."

Lavette eased the woman into her favorite chair and arranged a blanket on her lap. "Can I get you anything?"

"I would take a glass of water." Mrs. Sawyer smiled, the left side of her mouth sagging a little more than usual. "I seem to be parched after my nap." Lavette turned to leave when her mistress spoke again. "Oh, and you may show your young man in to see me."

"Yes, Ma'am."

Lavette almost tripped from excitement as she led Josiah into the parlor. "Mrs. Sawyer, this is Josiah Washington. He has a blacksmith shop here in town."

Josiah nodded in greeting, his hat lost in his hands. Mrs. Sawyer indicated the chair next to her, and he sat down. Lavette didn't know whether to leave or stay."

"If you don't mind, Ma'am, I'd like for Lavette to stay. What I have to say concerns her too."

Mrs. Sawyer glanced at Lavette, then back at Josiah. "That's fine with me. How can I help you? I believe you're the young man who rescued me yesterday. I thank you."

Josiah twisted his hat, his fingers kneading the material until Lavette thought it might rip into shreds. "I'm not sure if Lavette has mentioned me, Ma'am, but I've taken quite a liking to her." He hesitated and glanced at Lavette. "In fact, I love her very much."

Lavette put her hands to her warm

cheeks and couldn't look at her mistress. She'd had no idea Josiah would say something like this.

"I believe Lavette loves me, too, and I would like to speak with you about purchasing the remainder of her contract. I want her to be my wife, but I know Mr. Mead wouldn't allow that to happen."

"I don't know how you could know Mr. Mead's thoughts if you haven't spoken to him." Mrs. Sawyer's lips drew into a thin line, a sign that she wasn't happy. "The fact is, Mr. Mead has already proposed to buy her contract, should I choose to sell it."

"You mean you haven't actually agreed to let him?" Josiah looked hopeful. "If not, could you give me some time to raise what we need? I have some savings, and I'll work hard for the rest."

"Mr. Mead has agreed to pay me fifty dollars for Lavette's contract. Do you have that kind of money?" Mrs. Sawyer's imperious tone made Lavette clench her fists. How could she talk to Josiah like that?

"No, Ma'am, I don't have that much. Not even close." The sparkle in Josiah's eyes dimmed. He lowered his gaze. Bringing his head up, he smiled once more. "Could I give you what I have and make payments on the rest? I have friends who will vouch for me. I'm honest and I work hard. We could even postpone getting married until Lavette is free."

"That will never work. My son-in-law is using the money Mr. Mead is paying to build a room on his house for me. He needs that paid all at once so he will have the funds for the project."

Josiah nodded. Lavette wanted to cry. He'd tried his best, but it wasn't good enough.

"How do you even know Lavette wants to marry you? Have you asked her?" Mrs. Sawyer leaned forward in her chair.

"No, Ma'am, I haven't asked her yet, but I do know she loves me." He glanced over at Lavette. His eyes pleaded with her to return his love. She moved away from the door where she'd been standing and crossed the room. She knelt down at his feet, took one of his hands in hers, and squeezed. His love was almost visible in the air. She could feel it surrounding her.

"Ma'am, I'd be honored to be Josiah's wife. He's everything I've ever dreamed of." Lavette tore her gaze from Josiah's and looked at her mistress. Mrs. Sawyer frowned at them.

"I'll give you two weeks to earn the

money. If you haven't saved enough by then, I'll allow Mr. Mead to have her contract." She nodded, dismissing the two of them.

Tugging on Josiah's hand, Lavette urged him out of the room. This would never work. Fifty dollars was an unheard of amount for people like them. She would have to convince him to give up the idea of the two of them being together.

In the kitchen, she turned to him. He put his arms around her and hugged her to him. "Somehow, I'll get enough." His whispered promise only brought her pain.

"No." She too kept her voice low. "There's no way for you to do that. You have to give up the idea, Josiah. It won't work."

He stroked her hair, smoothing back the loosened tendrils. "You're a gift to me from God. I won't give up." He gave her a light kiss. "There's a man outside of Tucson who wants me to come out and do some work for him. I'll ride out there tomorrow. If he has some big jobs that pay well, I'll stay and do them."

"I wish I could help, but I have only a few dollars saved from my wages." Lavette rested her forehead on Josiah's broad chest. She longed to cling to him forever.

"I have an idea there, too."

"What?" Hope began to push away the doubts.

"Quinn mentioned the other day that Kathleen has more work than she can keep up with in her seamstress shop. With her time so close for the baby, she doesn't have the stamina she used to."

"Josiah Washington, you make her sound like a horse." Lavette giggled. "I can sew. I'll stop by tomorrow and see if she would like some help. I'm sure the pay won't be much, but I do want to help."

"I'd be happy to walk you over there tonight after Mrs. Sawyer goes to bed."

Lavette nodded, her heart full of love and hope for the first time she could remember.

Josiah couldn't help whistling as he turned up the path to Lavette's house. He could see her waiting in the shadows of the porch. Since Mrs. Sawyer always retired early, they had plenty of time to walk to Quinn and Kathleen's house. The thought of going anywhere with Lavette set his heart singing.

"There is a fountain filled with blood, drawn from Immanuel's veins." Lavette's voice rang out softly. He matched her volume since he didn't want to disturb Mrs. Sawyer.

He jumped onto the porch, ignoring the steps. He felt like he could leap to the moon and back tonight. "Good evenin', Beautiful." Lavette stopped singing. Her head dipped as if she were embarrassed. He wanted to grab her and kiss her again, but kept his hands at his sides.

"Evenin'."

"Ready to go?" Josiah stretched out a hand for hers. "I saw Quinn this afternoon and mentioned we might stop by."

She slipped her small hand into his. He sighed with pleasure at the touch. "I've decided that I need to teach you another verse of my fountain song on the way."

"I like the first two well enough. I'm ready for the third." Her eyes were dark in the twilight. "How many verses are there?"

"I know five. At church we don't always do all of them. Some of the folks have trouble remembering so many."

"Okay, I'm ready."

"Dear dying Lamb, Thy precious blood shall never lose its power, till all the ransomed Church of God, be saved, to sin no more: Be saved, to sin no more, be saved, to sin no more; till all the ransomed Church of God be saved to sin no more."

Josiah cleared his throat. Lavette walked in silence beside him.

"Okay, you've heard the words. Now join with me." He opened his mouth to sing, but something wasn't right. Lavette ignored him. A lone tear glistened on her cheek.

"Hey, what's wrong? Was I that bad?" He pulled her around, put a finger under her chin, and lifted.

Her mouth quivered. She tried to smile but failed. He put his arms around her, hugging her close. He couldn't think of anything he'd said or done to upset her, so he waited for her to gather her composure. When she was ready, she would tell him.

"I'm so sorry." Her arms slipped around his waist, and she leaned her cheek against him. "Those words showed me something I think Jesus has been trying to tell me."

"Well, I'm glad I didn't do anything wrong." Josiah gave her a light squeeze.

"No." She drew in a ragged breath. "You know I've been reading about Joseph. I've been angry with God so many years for allowing me to be a slave, that I didn't stop to think there are other forms of bondage than being in chains on a plantation. You tried to tell me that, too, didn't you?"

"Mm-hmm." Josiah leaned his cheek against the top of her head.

"Glorianna shared a verse with me the other day about being free in Jesus. That's what true freedom is, isn't it? Just like I can't pay the debt I owe Mrs. Sawyer, I can't pay the debt for my sins to God, either. Only Jesus could do that." She sniffed. He could feel her tears wetting his shirt.

"When I asked Jesus into my heart years ago, I was as free as I ever would be."

"There are many kinds of enslavement, and the worst is the bondage of sin." Josiah rubbed her back as he spoke. "I've never been a slave in the sense that you were, but for years I was bound in sin. I couldn't liberate myself. I had to have Jesus' help. He's the One who delivered me. I don't care if I'm put in chains for the rest of my life, I'll always be free because of Jesus paying the price for me."

"We're all ransomed like the words in that song say. By Jesus' blood we're set free." She wiped at her cheek. "I've wasted so many years being bitter and angry when all along what I wanted was already mine."

Cocking her head to the side, she frowned. "Another thing — I've always thought Jesus came for the white people. Now, I see He died for us all, didn't He?"

"That's right. He doesn't see any distinction in color or race. He loved us all enough to die for us."

She pushed back, and Josiah let his arms fall to his side. How he loved this woman. He planned to spend as many years as God gave him loving her and getting to know her better.

"We'd better get going, or the Kirbys may think we aren't coming." She held out a hand to him. "Let's do that verse again." She glanced up, and he could see the sheen of tears still in her eyes. "I may not be able to sing it aloud with you right now, but I'll be joining you inside."

Josiah set a leisurely pace as he began to sing once more. They repeated the hymn all the way to Quinn's house.

The rest of the evening sped past. Kathleen was grateful to Lavette for the offer of assistance. She wouldn't be able to pay much, but every penny would be put aside to add to what Josiah saved.

As they strolled home, Josiah couldn't help the melancholy that came over him. Tomorrow he would ride out to see Eduardo Villegas about the work he needed done. From what Eduardo told him, there was plenty to do. He probably wouldn't be back in town for at least a week. Not seeing Lavette for that long made him want to slow this evening down.

Back on the porch at Mrs. Sawyer's house, Josiah took Lavette in his arms one more time. He marveled at how tiny she felt. She was so perfect.

"I'll be leaving early in the morning."

"You've said that at least six times now." Her light tone told him she wasn't chiding him. "I know because every time you say that, I can't wait for you to return."

"You'll miss me then?" He brushed his lips over her forehead.

"Of course. Who else can teach me the words to the fountain hymn?" They both chuckled.

"I'll miss you more than I can say. As soon as I can, I'll get back to town. I'm hoping I'll have the money we need." He kissed her pert nose. "You start thinking about a wedding. Plan exactly what you want. I'm sure Glorianna and Kathleen will be glad to help."

"I don't care about a big wedding. I just want you." Lavette reached up and gave him a light kiss. "Hurry back. I'll be waiting."

As the door closed behind her, Josiah bounded off the porch. Eager to get going so he could return faster, he ran most of the way home.

Chapter 19

Heavy gray clouds hung low in the sky as Josiah rode into town twelve days later. Huge raindrops spattered against him, the warmth of the air making them feel like ice water. He ducked his head and pulled his hat down tight. Nothing could dampen his excitement at being back in Tucson with enough money to pay off Lavette's contract. By tomorrow morning, she would be free to be his wife. Working for Eduardo had taken more time than he figured, but the reward was earning enough for Lavette.

By the time he stabled his horse, darkness had fallen. The rain increased to a steady downpour unusual in this area, but welcomed to settle the dust. Josiah drew in a deep breath of the moisture-laden air. He'd never been fond of the downpours they had where he grew up, but now that he lived in the desert, he relished the infrequent showers.

Listening to the patter of drops outside, Josiah debated going to see Lavette tonight. He shook his head and sighed. It was late, and he needed some sleep. For close to two weeks, he'd worked long, hard hours. Eduardo had a nice forge already set up on his place. He'd said his father built it and knew how to do blacksmith work, but Eduardo never learned. With a sigh, Josiah blew out the lamp and climbed into bed, longing to see the woman he loved. He groaned. Every muscle in his body ached, but knowing Lavette would soon be his made all the discomfort worthwhile.

Clouds still draped across the sky in the morning. A light breeze gave a chill to the air, although the rain had ceased for the moment. Josiah loved the fresh-washed scent and breathed deeply. His heart raced faster than his feet as he headed to Lavette's. Safe at home, under the floor, was the money he'd earned. He wanted to speak with Mrs. Sawyer first and see when she wanted him to pay her. They would need to have some sort of paperwork done up to show that Lavette was free from her obligation to the elderly lady.

Josiah jumped onto the porch and rapped on the door. Before he could lower his hand, the door swung open. Lavette stood there, her eyes shining and wide, her whole countenance glowing. He swept her up and gave her a resounding kiss. Her arms tightened around his neck as she kissed him back.

"I thought you might not be coming back." She sounded breathless as he set her back on her feet.

"Eduardo had more work for me than I thought. I hurried as fast as I could." He cupped her soft cheek in his hand, unable to resist the contact. His eyes drank in her beauty. "I've missed you so much."

She caught his hand in hers and kissed his fingers. "I've missed you too. Come on in. I've got some fresh cinnamon buns."

Stepping inside, Josiah could smell the heavenly aroma of the sweets. "Mmm." His stomach growled, and he gave Lavette a sheepish grin. "I didn't eat breakfast this morning. I wanted to get over here and see you first."

She laughed and pulled him toward the kitchen. "Come on. I'll make you something to eat." She held a finger to her lips. "We'll have to be quiet. Mrs. Sawyer is still sleeping."

He sat at the table and watched her break eggs into a skillet. The chunk of bacon she'd thrown in sizzled. Contentment washed over him. He could imagine how wonderful life would be when he and Lavette were married. Every morning he would wake up to her beautiful face, and every night he would go to sleep with her beside him.

Lavette set a plate of food in front of him and dropped into the chair on the other side of the table. "I can't wait any longer. Tell me about your work for this Eduardo."

Josiah's mouth dropped open. Shame washed over him. "I'm sorry. How could I have been so thoughtless?" He reached over and took her hands in his. "I have the money."

Her face lit up with a mixture of surprise and joy.

"Here? Did you bring it today?"

"No, I have it safe at my place. I wasn't sure how Mrs. Sawyer wanted to do this. I need to talk to her."

Tears rolled down Lavette's cheeks. She pulled her hands free and wiped the drops away with the edge of her apron. "This is so silly of me." She sniffed. "I didn't want to believe you could earn enough. I only managed to get three dollars from the work I did for Kathleen. How did you get so much?"

Standing, Josiah pulled Lavette up into his embrace. He stroked her slender back, trying to comfort her. "I had some put by already. Eduardo has a lot of horses, but shoeing doesn't pay much. I rebuilt a couple of old wagons for him. That's what paid off." He tipped Lavette's head back and gazed into her bright eyes. "You save what you earned and buy something for yourself. Maybe you could use it for material to make a new dress for our wedding."

"I can't recall ever having a new dress of my own." Lavette gave him a fierce hug. A bell tinkled. She jumped. "Mrs. Sawyer is awake." She pushed Josiah toward the chair. "You sit down and eat that breakfast. The cinnamon buns are on the stove. Help yourself. I'll let you know when we're ready for you."

Josiah watched her rush from the room. He'd never seen Lavette so flustered. She reminded him of a bird trapped in a building, fluttering to and fro, trying to find a way out. He shoveled a bite of eggs and bacon into his mouth. Life with Lavette would be pure joy.

Lavette took most of an hour getting Mrs. Sawyer ready for company. Josiah ate more sweet rolls than he should have while waiting. He was used to working, not sitting patiently. He needed to be doing something.

When Lavette finally escorted him into the parlor, Mrs. Sawyer was sitting in the chair by the window. Her erect posture and stern demeanor told him she wasn't happy to see him.

"Good morning, Ma'am." Josiah gave her a polite nod.

She inclined her head but didn't ask him to sit down. "Lavette said you wish to speak with me again. What is it this time?"

Surprised, Josiah stayed silent for a moment. "I've earned the money needed to purchase Lavette's contract. I came to see how you would like to do this."

"Isn't the time I extended to you already up?" Her cold gaze sent a chill through him.

"I believe you gave me two weeks, Ma'am. Tomorrow would be the last day." Josiah forced himself to stand quietly. He refused to let this woman know how she rattled him with her obvious wish to sell Lavette to Mead.

She nodded. "Mr. Mead and I both believed you would not be able to come up with the money. He plans to be here today with the papers for me to look over. Then, tomorrow the transaction will be final."

"But you gave your word." Lavette's voice shook as she spoke. Josiah could hear the hopelessness in her undertone.

Mrs. Sawyer gave Lavette a hard look. "I'm doing this for your good, Lavette. I have come to care for you over the years."

"If you care for me at all, you'll let Josiah, not Mr. Mead, have me." Lavette twisted her fingers together. Josiah longed to comfort her.

"I'm not at all sure that would be to your benefit. I have heard some rather disparaging things about Mr. Washington's character and background. Until I'm positive he will care for you properly, I can't let you go with him."

"What things have you heard?" Lavette and Josiah spoke at the same time. Josiah glanced at her and could see the disbelief and anger that matched his own.

Mrs. Sawyer studied them both for several minutes. "I have heard that Mr. Washington left the East to join the cavalry because of some trouble he got into. Trouble with the law, I might add."

"That can't be true." Lavette's eyes were wide as she stared at him. Josiah was too stunned to speak.

"Do you have anything to say for yourself, young man?"

"Ma'am, the closest thing I've ever done to a crime was when I was five. I stole a pie my mother had cooling on the windowsill. I ate the whole thing and got sick. My mama said the sickness was a punishment for stealing. I never did that again."

"And how am I supposed to believe that?" Mrs. Sawyer's tone could freeze the sun in the sky.

"I don't know how I can prove myself, Ma'am. All I can say is that I'm a Christian, and I try to live a godly life according to the Bible. I don't know where you heard these stories, but they aren't true."

"Are you saying my very reliable sources are lying?"

"No, Ma'am, I'm saying they are mistaken. They must have gotten the wrong information or the wrong person."

"Mrs. Sawyer, I've never met such a kind, caring man as Josiah. I know he couldn't have done those things." Lavette stepped closer and put her hand on Josiah's arm, as if to add her word to his.

"Can you bring me someone who can vouch for you — someone upstanding in the community?" From her tone, Josiah knew Mrs. Sawyer doubted he could do that.

"Yes, Ma'am, I have a lot of friends here."

"Then you may return tomorrow with

your money and your friend." She paused and Josiah turned to leave. "Oh, and Mr. Washington."

He turned back. "Yes, Ma'am."

"Your friend should be someone I'll have no doubts about."

His boots clumped out a rhythm of doom as Josiah crossed to the door. Where had Mrs. Sawyer heard those rumors? His lips thinned to an angry line. Mead. Who else would bother to tarnish his reputation? Lavette trudged behind him in forlorn silence. She held the door as he stepped out. When she looked at him, he could see the despair in her eyes that matched the feelings in him. He held her close and kissed her forehead, wondering if this were one of the last times he would be allowed such a privilege.

"Remember Joseph, Josiah? God always saw him through the times when there didn't seem to be any hope."

"I know, Honey. I'll see you tomorrow." He gave her a quick kiss and stalked down the path. He had some errands to run, then he would work. When he was angry, only talking to God and hard work seemed to bring release.

Lavette knelt beside her bed, her Bible

on her lap, open to the book of Genesis. The lamp on the floor beside her cast a circle of light around her. She rested her forehead against the blanket.

"Lord Jesus, help me. I feel like Joseph in the pit, waiting for his brothers to sell him into slavery. You know what will happen if Mr. Mead gets my contract. You know the things I'll be required to do — things that don't honor You. Jesus, I want to run away, but I'm trusting You to work everything out instead. I know Josiah is a good man. He loves You. He loves me too. Please help us. Make Mrs. Sawyer see the truth tomorrow."

She clutched the Bible to her breast, thinking how far she'd come. The thought of slavery didn't scare her so much any-more. She knew Jesus wanted the best for her, and anything that happened would be to His glory. The long talks she'd had with Kathleen over the last two weeks had helped her understand so much about the Bible and the way Christians were to be-lieve. As long as she had Jesus in her heart, she would have the freedom she desired, and the Bible said no one could take Him away from her.

A light tapping at the front door snapped her head up. Josiah? Would he come by this late to see her? Jumping up, she reached for her wrapper. Her bare feet made little noise on the hallway floor. She lifted the latch, her heart thundering in anticipation of seeing the very man she'd been thinking about.

"Good evening, my sweet." Bertrand Mead sagged against the doorjamb, his breath laden with alcohol. Lavette swung the door to slam it shut, but he put his foot in the way.

"Now is that any way to treat your prospective owner?" He grabbed her, his fingers digging into her shoulder. "In the good days before the war, when a man bought slaves, he got to examine them thoroughly. I think I should get the same privilege, don't you?"

"Let me go. You're drunk." Lavette jerked back, but she couldn't break his hold.

"Now, now, my sweet, don't fight me." Mead tugged at the sash on her wrapper.

"Stop that, or I'll scream."

"And who would care about a slave girl screaming?" He chuckled, a malevolent sound that sent chills racing down Lavette's spine.

"I am not a slave. Let me go."

"I'm buying you, aren't I? When I pay

my money tomorrow, you'll be mine."

"You won't get to do that." She spat the words at him. "Josiah earned enough. He'll be here in the morning to purchase my contract. You don't have a chance."

His lip lifted in a sneer. He yanked her tight against him. "Your Josiah doesn't stand a chance. A man of his ilk wouldn't be good for a girl like you. You need a man of sterling character like me." He lowered his mouth. Lavette turned her head, and he gave her a slobbery kiss on the cheek. She stomped on his boot, but her bare foot made no impression. He chuckled.

A sob welled up inside her. *Jesus, help me.* She pushed again. Mead stumbled back. He let go. His arms flailed as he teetered on the edge of the porch. Lavette darted into the house, shut the door, and slid the bolt home. Her whole body trembled as she strained to hear if he was gone. What if he tried to force the door or get in a window? Her heart thundered.

Uneven steps clumped to the door. Mead's voice came clearly through the cracks. "I know you're in there, my sweet. The wait will make our time tomorrow night more delightful. Think about that."

She listened to his uneven tread. Silence hung heavy like a shroud. She covered her mouth to hold back the sobs. What would tomorrow bring? Could she trust Jesus with this? *Lord, help me.* She cried the words from the depth of her soul. A comforting warmth settled about her. She basked in the feeling of contentment. This must be the peace Kathleen told her about, the peace that passed all understanding. She moved down the hall with lighter steps. With Jesus watching over her, she would sleep well tonight.

Chapter 20

Cavelike darkness surrounded Josiah as he stepped from his smithy. Glancing back, he could see the faint glow from the banked coals. Although he'd spent hours working, he still didn't have the tranquillity he longed for. He was in turmoil over what would happen with Lavette. His body couldn't continue. Exhausted after this day and the long days he'd put in for nearly two weeks, he shuffled around the side of the building.

Heavy clouds blocked the moon and stars, so nothing lit the night. He hadn't bothered with a lantern. The path to his door was as familiar as the back of his hand. The dark didn't trouble him. He fumbled in the pitch black for the latch to his door.

Josiah paused. The door wasn't latched. With a slight creak, it swung open. He couldn't hear anything. Had he left the door open by accident? When he'd returned from speaking with Mrs. Sawyer, he'd been so distraught, he might have done anything. He stepped inside.

Pain exploded in his head. Josiah fell back against the wall. Something whooshed past him and thudded on the side of the door close to his ear. He pushed against the wood. The world was spinning. Bile rose in his throat. He fell. Something hard struck him in the back of the head. He pitched forward. Darkness closed around him. All sound faded.

The soft coo of a mourning dove awakened Josiah. The sound echoed in his head like a gunshot. He tried to open his eyes. The gray light of dawn pierced like a needle. He groaned. As he pushed up from the floor, the world began to tilt. His stomach roiled. Blackness surrounded him, and he sank into oblivion.

"Josiah." Someone's hand lifted his shoulder, rattling his brains. "Josiah, can you hear me?"

He groaned. Bright light sent a pain to the base of his skull. He closed his eyes.

"Josiah, I'm going for help. You stay still." The voice that sounded like Conlon quieted, and Josiah drifted off once more.

He awoke again to someone prodding the sore spot on his temple. He squinted and could see Doc Meyer, Conlon, and Quinn hovering over him.

"Good thing he has a hard head." Doc grunted. "I don't feel anything cracked. He'll need a little rest, then he'll be fine." Pulling out some cloth, he began to bandage Josiah's wounds. He stood, dusted off his pants, and picked up his bag from the floor next to Josiah.

"Thanks, Doc." Josiah barely got the words out. He licked his dry lips with a tongue that felt like a rolled-up sock.

"Let me get you some water." Conlon patted Josiah's leg. Josiah did his best to stifle a groan.

"What happened?" He spoke to Quinn, who still knelt beside him.

"I think you were robbed. I'm guessing you came home and surprised the thief. He hit you with this." Quinn held up a poker.

"I always did say you were thick headed for a reason." Conlon knelt beside him and gave him a sip of cool water. Josiah took a second drink and eased up to a sitting position. The room swam in sickening circles. He closed his eyes until the dizziness passed, then opened them slowly.

"My money." He tried to stand, but Quinn pushed him back.

"Oh, no, you don't. You sit right there until you get your bearings." Quinn glanced at Conlon, then met Josiah's gaze. "Did you keep the money you earned in a box under a floorboard?" Josiah nodded and winced. Quinn frowned. "The board's been pulled up, and the hole is empty. Did you get a look at who hit you?"

"No." Josiah's fingers probed the knot on the back of his skull. "It was pitch black last night. I didn't have a lantern. He was in the house when I came in. I didn't even see him coming."

Quinn blew out a breath. "I think we all know who's responsible, but proving that will be difficult." Josiah saw Conlon nod.

"You need to rest, Josiah. We'll help you into bed, then Quinn and I will ask around town to see what we can find out. We'll come by right after lunch and go with you to Mrs. Sawyer's, like we planned."

Josiah had talked to Quinn and Conlon yesterday about being his character witnesses before Mrs. Sawyer. They both agreed and made arrangements to meet at her house this afternoon. Now, he wondered if they should bother.

"I can't go there. If I haven't got any money to buy the contract, how will I face Lavette?"

"She deserves to know what happened." Conlon squeezed Josiah's shoulder. "She's quite a girl. Give her a chance."

After Conlon and Quinn left, Josiah couldn't stop the tears that seeped from his eyes. "Jesus, I've made a mess of things. All along, I assumed my being with Lavette was Your will. I didn't stop to ask what You wanted me to do. I barged ahead on my own. Please, Lord, don't let Lavette suffer for my willfulness. Work this out according to Your plan and Your will. Thank You, Jesus." Josiah drifted into a restful sleep, marveling at the peace he felt inside, when all around him things were in turmoil.

Lavette swung the door open before Josiah finished knocking. She'd heard a wagon draw up outside. Looking out the window, she'd seen a strange sight. Conlon was helping Josiah down as Quinn tied the horses. Why had they come in a wagon? What was wrong with Josiah? Her heart pounded as she raced to greet them.

"Josiah, what's wrong?" She gripped the door, fear clutching at her as she took in the sight of the white bandage on Josiah's temple. He didn't give her his usual smile.

"Someone robbed me last night." He touched the bandage. "They tried to dent my skull but failed." His lips trembled as he tried to smile. "I need to talk with Mrs. Sawyer. I don't have the money we need."

"Oh, Josiah, it doesn't matter." Lavette traced the side of his cheek with her fingers. "I'm so glad you're all right. I know everything else will work out fine."

Josiah nodded. Lavette stepped back for them to enter, embarrassed at her temerity in front of Josiah's friends. They didn't seem to mind. In fact, the two men seemed pleased as they followed Josiah inside. Lavette led the way to the front room. Mrs. Sawyer was already up from her nap and seated by the open window.

"Good afternoon, gentlemen." Mrs. Sawyer looked surprised to see the deputy sheriff and a cavalry lieutenant accompanying Josiah. She gestured to the other chairs in the room, and the men seated themselves.

"Mrs. Sawyer, I brought two of my friends to vouch for my character." Josiah's voice was full of anguish. Lavette stood behind him and placed her hands on his shoulders. He reached up and squeezed her fingers.

"You look as though you've been in a fight. I thought perhaps you were under arrest."

Quinn chuckled and Conlon grinned.

"No, Ma'am." Quinn spoke up. "Josiah is one of the finest men you'll ever meet. I can't imagine him being arrested for anything."

"That's right." Conlon winked at Josiah. "I've known him for several years now. We met when he was still in the cavalry. He's a godly man and one you can trust completely."

Mrs. Sawyer sat quiet, studying the two men. She looked at Josiah. "I guess I can have no further objections to you then. I have the papers in my room. Have you brought the money?"

Lavette felt Josiah's shoulders sag. "No, Ma'am. I don't have it."

"Then you lied to me yesterday? You said you'd earned enough and would bring it today."

"I intended to, but last night I was robbed."

Mrs. Sawyer frowned and started to reply. Before she could say anything, footsteps echoed on the porch, followed by knocking. Lavette slipped from the parlor. She opened the door to find Mead waiting, a twisted grin on his face. Understanding dawned. She knew this man was responsible for what had happened to Josiah. She stepped out and shut the door. She moved down the porch closer to the open window.

Josiah's heart ached as Lavette left the room. That must be Mead. In a few minutes, Lavette would belong to that scoundrel. Josiah couldn't do anything to rescue her now.

Mrs. Sawyer opened her mouth to say something, then stopped. She cocked her head to one side. Josiah could see Conlon and Quinn frowning in concentration. He began to listen.

From the open window, he heard Bertrand Mead speaking. "I'm glad you're so eager to see me this morning. After my reception last night, I thought you might give me trouble today."

"Josiah is here. What makes you think I'll be yours? He earned the money to buy my contract."

"So you said last night, my sweet. I thank you for that helpful bit of information." Mead's words made Josiah clench his fists. "I know he won't be able to come up with the funds he needs."

"And how would you know that?"

"Oh, I have my ways, sweet thing." The boards outside the window creaked. "Why don't you and I go inside and get this business taken care of? Then you can come with me and begin learning how to entertain."

"You said you wanted me to sing. I already know how to do that." Lavette's voice held steady.

"Oh, I intend for you to sing, but I also have other plans for you, my sweet. With your beauty, men will pay a lot. I'm going to make a fortune off of you." Mead chuckled.

Mrs. Sawyer gave a slight gasp.

"You're too late. Josiah is talking with Mrs. Sawyer right now."

"Oh, but he won't have the money he needs." Mead chuckled.

"How do you know that?"

"Because I went to his place and made sure of it last night." The threat in Mead's tone made Josiah tremble with the desire to protect Lavette. "In fact, if it hadn't been so dark, he wouldn't be here at all."

"You would have killed him?" Lavette's gasp drowned out Mrs. Sawyer's.

"Yes," Mead hissed.

Quinn stood and lifted his revolver from the holster. He gave Mrs. Sawyer a long look and stepped from the room. Josiah could hear the front door opening and the creak of the boards as the deputy strode to where Mead and Lavette stood outside the window.

"I believe I owe you an apology, Mr. Washington." Mrs. Sawyer sounded tired. She rubbed her forehead. "When you get the money back from Mr. Mead, come by to see me."

Josiah nodded and followed Conlon from the room.

"Are you ready?" Josiah spoke close to Lavette's ear, sending a shiver of delight through her.

"Josiah, this is silly. Take this blindfold off." Lavette blinked in the bright light as Josiah whisked the cloth away from her eyes. She gasped in delight. There in front of her was a new cottage. She could smell the cut wood on the porch. The rest of the house was made from adobe bricks.

"Come on." Josiah dragged her up the stairs and opened the door.

She stepped inside and marveled at the newness of everything. The kitchen had a stove, newly blacked, shelves with dishes, and pans hanging on the walls. A small table stood at one side. Josiah led her through the rest of the house, grinning at her delight.

"This is our room." He opened the door to the bedroom, and she walked in. White curtains fluttered at the window. A colorful rag rug covered the floor by the bed. What caught her eye, though, was the yellow dress hanging on the wall.

"Oh, Josiah, it's beautiful."

"The dress is a gift from Kathleen. She and Glorianna thought you would look pretty in yellow." He wrapped his arms around her and whispered in her ear. "I think you're beautiful in any color."

"How did you manage this?" Lavette turned in Josiah's arms to face him.

"You can thank Mrs. Sawyer." He grinned. "When I went to pay her the money for your contract, she refused to take any. She asked me where we would live, and when I told her about the room by the smithy, she insisted I use the contract money to build you a house. She said you deserved the best for all you'd given up." He planted a kiss on her nose. "She's right, you know. She also said your freedom would be our wedding gift from her. Paul didn't need the money anymore since she decided to return to Virginia."

"This is like a dream come true."

"I was worried I wouldn't get done before our wedding tomorrow, but other than a few finishing touches, the house is ready to move into."

"You are amazing, Josiah Washington. You're the handsome prince I always dreamed about."

"And you're the sweetheart I never thought I'd get. I love you more than I can say, Lavette. I look forward to spending a lifetime with you."

As Josiah's lips met hers, Lavette couldn't stop the prayer of thankfulness for all the Lord had given her. She'd wanted freedom, and He'd given so much more.

About the Author

Nancy J. Farrier resides in Arizona. She is married and the mother of one son and four daughters. She is the author of numerous articles and short stories. She homeschools her three youngest daughters and writes in the evenings. Nancy enjoys sharing her faith through her writing.